WHERE DREAMS COME TRUE

The Daily Cruise Letter/The Daily Cruise News

Join Captain Nikolas Pappas and his staff for the most memorable night of our sailing! Tonight is the Neptune Ball, a gala extravaganza that is one of the highlights of a cruise on *Alexandra's Dream*.

You'll be transported back to the glamour days of luxury cruise ship travel. Dance to the sounds of big band tunes, dine on our chef's finest gourmet creations and toast the pleasures of life with a glass of bubbly. This is the night for ball gowns, tiaras and tuxes. Life at sea provides an escape from the real world, and as we float beneath the starry skies, the mysteries of the Mediterranean will work their magic.

Let yourself fall in love again this cruise—with your husband, your wife, your family, or life itself. Passengers June and Albert Westcott have announced that after sixty years of marriage, they are planning to renew their vows in a ceremony in the Court of Dreams this Friday. What greater proof can there be that romance is alive and well on *Alexandra's Dream!*

CINDI MYERS

Cindi Myers became one of the most popular people in eighth grade when she and her best friend wrote a torrid historical romance and circulated it among their peers. Fame was short-lived, however; the English teacher confiscated the manuscript and advised her to concentrate on learning to properly diagram a sentence. From this humbling beginning she has gone on to write over two dozen novels. Her books have been Waldenbooks bestsellers and have been praised for their emotion, humor and sensuality. She writes stories about relationships that matter, whether the subject is female friendship, families, or the love between a man and a woman.

Mediterranean
N I G H T S™

Cindi Myers

A PERFECT MARRIAGE?

HARLEQUIN®

TORONTO • NEW YORK • LONDON
AMSTERDAM • PARIS • SYDNEY • HAMBURG
STOCKHOLM • ATHENS • TOKYO • MILAN • MADRID
PRAGUE • WARSAW • BUDAPEST • AUCKLAND

ISBN-13: 978-0-373-38966-7
ISBN-10:   0-373-38966-3

A PERFECT MARRIAGE?

Copyright © 2007 by Harlequin Books S.A.

Cynthia S. Myers is acknowledged as the author of this work.

Dear Reader,

I'm so excited to be part of this great MEDITERRANEAN NIGHTS continuity series. I've enjoyed following the adventures of everyone on board *Alexandra's Dream,* and being a part of their stories.

I was especially pleased to write Katherine and Charles's story. Like Katherine, I married young and have been married many years. In all the busyness of raising children and handling careers, it's easy for romance to take a backseat. As Katherine and Charles prove, the effort to keep that romance alive is well worth it.

Which is why I love romance novels and romance readers. You are keeping romance alive in your lives every day. I'd love to hear from you. Drop me a line at Cindi@CindiMyers.com or write to me at P.O. Box 991, Bailey, CO 80421.

Best,

Cindi Myers

For Julie and Ken

DON'T MISS THE STORIES OF

Mediterranean
N I G H T S™

CHAPTER ONE

"A CRUISE. A CRUISE is just what you and Charles need. Spend a few days relaxing at sea and you'll realize there's nothing wrong with your marriage some time together won't put right."

Her father's words returned to Katherine Stamos as she stood on the deck of *Alexandra's Dream,* watching the Piraeus skyline grow smaller and smaller. The sounds of joy and celebration surrounded her, but inside she felt hollow, like an outsider invited to a stranger's party. While everyone else was excited to be embarking on a dream vacation, she faced the voyage filled with doubt. Could twelve days cruising in the Mediterranean really bridge the distance between her and her husband that had been brewing for years?

She searched the faces of those crowded along the rail until she spotted Charles. He stood with Gideon Dayan, the ship's Chief Security Officer, no doubt engrossed in discussing some architectural aspect of the shrinking Piraeus skyline.

As she watched, Charles gestured toward the shore and she smiled, pleased that, after nineteen years, she knew him that well at least. Charles's passion for archi-lecture was one of the things that made him so successful in the field—a success that meant he spent weeks every month traveling to various projects around the world.

As if feeling her gaze on him, he turned and flashed a smile that, even now, made her heart skip a beat. Tall and slender, with sandy brown hair slightly receding from his high forehead and blue eyes that sparkled with intelligence and wit, he was the kind of man others instinctively turned to for advice and help. The kind of man any woman would be proud to call her husband.

But there had to be more to marriage than pride in a partner's accomplishments and appearance or even the pleasant companionship she and Charles still enjoyed. There ought to be more passion…more joy.

"Oh, love, isn't this the most thrilling day, ever?" The woman next to Katherine, a diminutive apple-cheeked doll with a platinum coronet of braids atop her head, squeezed the hand of the silver-haired gentleman beside her.

"It is, indeed, dear," the man replied, smiling fondly at the woman.

She beamed at Katherine. "I could hardly sleep last night, I was so excited," she said.

"We're certainly starting with beautiful weather," Katherine said. Sun sparkled silver on sapphire water beneath a cloudless sky. No artist's rendering of paradise could compare with the beauty before them.

"Have you been on a cruise before?" the woman asked.

"Yes, I've been on a few cruises." No need to mention that her father owned the cruise line, or that her job as head of public relations for the line had led her to spend quite a bit of time on *Alexandra's Dream*, though this was her first trip primarily in the role of passenger.

"Then, I may be looking you up if I have questions." The woman offered a plump hand. "I'm June Westcott and this is my husband, Albert."

"Pleased to meet you." She shook hands with each of them. "I'm Katherine Stamos. My husband, Charles Slater, is the tall man over by the lifeboats, the one talking to the security officer."

June obligingly looked toward Charles, who was still engrossed in his conversation. "Ooh, he's quite handsome!" She turned back to Katherine. "The two of you make a very good-looking couple."

"Thank you." She glanced at their joined hands. She hadn't failed to notice how Albert's gaze continually strayed to his wife, his look adoring. Were the two of them perhaps on their honeymoon, the result of a golden-age romance? "How long have you been married?" she asked.

"Sixty years this month," Albert said. He put his arm around June and pulled her closer. "We met when I was a soldier stationed at Bristol."

"I was the cigarette girl at the canteen," June said. "He would come in with his mates and spend all his time flirting with me."

"She had the best legs in London," he said. "And the sauciest tongue."

"He was the handsomest man in the place," she said, smiling up at him. "Once I laid eyes on him, I never looked at anyone else. I had to have him."

In a younger couple, such open adoration might have been cloying, but the devotion of this pair was so genuine and unaffected, Katherine couldn't help but smile, even as envy pinched at her heart. What she wouldn't give to have Charles look at her with such unabashed love. Had he ever regarded her that way, or was it only in her imagination that he had? Memory tended to tint things a rosy hue, making the present suffer more by comparison.

"Ooh, look, love, is that the hotel where we stayed last night?" June stood on tiptoe and leaned over the rail. "It looks so different from here."

"All the buildings look so white," Albert said. "Don't see how they keep them so clean."

"It's the limestone tufa used to construct them."

Charles joined them at the rail. "The crystals in it reflect the light, making it appear very white."

"June and Albert, this is my husband, Charles. Charles, this is June and Albert Westcott." Katherine made the introductions. "The Westcotts are celebrating their sixtieth anniversary."

"Congratulations." Charles shook hands with the older couple. "Sixty years is quite an accomplishment, these days."

"We both feel very blessed," June said. She squeezed her husband's hand.

"It was good to meet you both," Albert said, nodding to each of them. "I think we'll head to our cabin now and get settled in."

"Gideon told me they'll be having the lifeboat drill soon," Charles said.

"Oh, Albert, we'd better go," June said. "I want to get a place up front so I can hear everything." She fluttered her fingers at Katherine and Charles. "I hope to see you two later."

As she and Albert turned away and were swallowed up by the crowd making its way toward the elevators, Katherine heard June ask, "Do you think they'll need volunteers? I've always wondered what it would be like to ride in one of those little boats."

"They seem like a lively pair," Charles remarked.

"Yes," Katherine said. "Do you think we'll be like that when we're their age?"

"I can't see you volunteering to assist with the lifeboat drill, no." He chuckled and put his hand at her back. "Come on, let's check out our quarters."

She wanted to tell him she hadn't been talking about the lifeboat drill, but, if he didn't already realize that, what was the point?

They took the elevator up to their penthouse suite. Decorated in warm tones of white, gold and olive, the suite was the epitome of understated luxury. Katherine sank onto the white leather love seat and admired the photographs of the Acropolis and the Parthenon that decorated the opposite wall. Their father had asked Katherine's younger sister, Helena, to oversee the interior design of all the rooms and she had done a superb job.

"My mother would have loved this room," Katherine said. "She would have loved everything about this ship, I think." A familiar ache pinched at her; even after ten years, she still missed her mother terribly.

"This whole ship is a tribute to your mother, isn't it?" Charles sat beside her on the love seat. "A floating memorial."

"I suppose it is." Only recently had her father, Elias, truly emerged from the cloud of grief that had engulfed him after his wife's death, even though it had been almost ten years ago. Katherine had taken for granted that he mourned so deeply because he loved Alexandra so much. But the revelation that Elias had a son, Theo, by another woman, had shaken that belief. Apparently, Alexandra had known about Theo and made her peace with the idea, but, for Katherine and Helena, the news had been a great shock. Granted, Theo had been conceived before Elias's engagement to Alexandra, but could it be that part of Elias's pain was caused by guilt?

"I had an interesting conversation with Gideon," Charles said. He settled back on the love seat, one arm stretched out behind her.

"Oh? What about?" she asked, only half interested, her mind still on her father and her memories of her mother. Alexandra had been the perfect, devoted wife. Always supportive, an excellent hostess, a loving mother. Her reward had been a husband who adored her.

"He was telling me about some of what's happened on previous cruises of this boat."

"It's a ship, dear." Katherine turned her attention to Charles. "The crew won't take kindly to your calling it a boat."

"Yes, well, Gideon said some stolen artifacts were found hidden on board during the ship's very first sailing."

"Yes. My father was very upset. You know how passionate he is about preserving Greece's treasures." Elias had contributed generously to many preservation efforts and was known as a vocal opponent of any attempts—legal or illegal—to remove important artifacts from their country of origin.

"I'm sure he was," Charles said. "Gideon is convinced it was an isolated incident, but other disturbing things have happened, as well. Last month, the ship's librarian disappeared while the ship was in port."

"I told you that," she said. Was there some sort of male gene that automatically filtered out half of what their wives said? "Ariana Bennett went missing while the ship was docked in Naples. Does Gideon think her disappearance and the stolen antiquities are connected?"

Charles shook his head. "No. But he does believe she chose not to return. Supposedly the woman was involved with the first officer, Giorgio something-or-other. It's thought she had an argument and ran off rather than have to face the rest of the crew."

"Tzekas. It's Giorgio Tzekas. And that's just gossip. I'm not sure I believe it." The handsome first officer was the son of her father's best friend, and she knew enough about him to be unimpressed. Even as a boy Giorgio had been spoiled, lazy and arrogant. She had seen no signs that age had improved him any. "Giorgio is the type of man who likes to imagine that every woman is ready to fall at his feet. But his first love will always be Giorgio himself."

"Did you meet Ariana when you were on the ship before?" Charles asked.

"Yes. She seemed very nice. Quiet. Very intelligent. She didn't strike me as the impulsive type." Or the type to be taken in by a womanizer like Giorgio.

"Maybe that's because you're not impulsive, yourself," Charles said.

Was that a criticism? Did he want her to be more impulsive? "I wouldn't say you are, either," she said.

He smiled and shook his head. "No, I'm not. I guess that makes us two of a kind."

"Hmm." When they were first married, she would have said she and Charles were a great deal alike, both optimistic, ambitious people with the same goals and ideals. Was that still true after all these years?

She had been only nineteen when she met Charles, a girl from a privileged family who had led a sheltered life. Four years older and already making his own way in the world, Charles had represented a kind of independence Katherine had never known. She had fallen quickly and deeply in love, and even her father's initial disapproval of the match had done nothing to lessen her determination to spend the rest of her life with Charles.

This cruise was her chance to discover if the qualities that had initially drawn her and Charles to each other still bound them together.

Anyone observing them would have probably said they had a good marriage. They seldom argued. Charles was unfailingly polite. Though he traveled a great deal for his work, Katherine believed he was faithful.

But, though they respected one another and got along well enough, it had been a long time since Katherine had felt any real connection with her husband.

The spark of desire that had once made her long to be with him, the feeling that he was her best friend and closest confidant, had been replaced by a vague indifference. She looked at him at times and saw a polite stranger—a man with whom she shared a home and a child, but little else. The knowledge filled her with sadness.

Alarm bells sounded and passengers were ordered to report to their lifeboat stations. "I'll get the life vests," Charles said, heading for the bedroom.

They joined the crowd at the stairs headed for the lifeboats. Katherine spotted June and Albert, each wearing a bright orange life preserver. June was smiling and chatting with another woman, obviously thrilled by even the routine of the drill.

"Excuse me. Am I headed the right way for the lifeboats?" An attractive fiftyish woman with light brown hair and blue eyes squeezed in beside them.

"You're headed in the right direction," Charles said. "Just follow the crowd."

"Oh, good." The woman smiled. She looked tired and there was a sadness in her eyes that belied the smile on her lips. "I'm Sadie Bennett," she said.

The name struck a chord with Katherine. "Are you related to Ariana Bennett?" she asked.

The woman's smile faded altogether and she nodded. "Ariana is my daughter. Do you know her?"

"I met her once before when I was on the ship. I'm Katherine Stamos and this is my husband, Charles Slater." She put a hand on Charles's arm. "This is Ariana Bennett's mother. The ship's librarian I told you about."

"I was sorry to hear that Ariana had left the ship," Charles said. "Have you heard from her?"

"No. Nothing." Sadie looked away as they descended another flight of stairs, then emerged onto a deck amid rows of white-and-orange lifeboats. A white-coated steward directed them where to stand and, for the next few minutes, they practiced donning their life vests and learned what to do in case of an emergency.

When the drill ended, Katherine and Charles turned to make their way back to their rooms, but a hand on Katherine's arm stopped her. She turned to see Sadie Bennett beside her. "I'm sorry to disturb you," Sadie said, "but I wondered if I might ask you a few questions."

"I'll meet you in the room," Charles said, taking Katherine's life vest from her.

"All right." She had really hoped to begin the cruise on the right foot, perhaps with a celebratory toast in their room, some quiet conversation on their private deck…maybe even an afternoon of lovemaking in the inviting king-sized bed. But the sadness in Sadie Bennett's eyes made it impossible for Katherine to refuse the woman's request. After all, she was a mother, herself. How would she feel if her daughter, Gemma, suddenly vanished without a trace?

"Let's go to the tearoom," Katherine said. "It should be quiet there, and we can talk."

The two women said nothing as they made their way to the Rose Petal tearoom on the Bacchus deck. As Katherine had hoped, the small restaurant was empty, and they settled into two chintz chairs at a dark wood table. A waiter immediately appeared. "Would you like tea?" Katherine asked.

Sadie shook her head. "No thank you."

"Nothing right now," Katherine said. When the waiter was gone, she turned to Sadie. "What can I do for you?"

Sadie smoothed her skirt across her knees and leveled a calm gaze at Katherine. "You said your last name is Stamos. Are you related to Elias Stamos?"

"Yes, he's my father."

Sadie nodded. "He's the one who told me about Ariana's disappearance. I was impressed that the owner of a cruise line would take it upon himself to do so."

"My father was very upset when he learned that Ariana failed to return to the ship in Naples," Katherine said. "He's doing everything in his power to find out what happened to her." Elias had even hired a local investigator to try to track down the missing librarian, with no luck.

Sadie leaned forward, her hands clasped tightly in her lap. "You said you met Ariana. What kind of mood was she in when you saw her? Was she happy? Did she seem upset about anything at all?"

"I didn't really know her that well," Katherine hedged. "She didn't seem…unhappy. She struck me as a quiet young woman. Very intelligent and serious."

Sadie nodded. "Yes, that's Ariana. She's always loved books, especially anything to do with Greek and Roman history and art." She smiled sadly. "It was an interest she and her father shared. After he passed away earlier this year, she became determined to see all the places he'd visited and had told her about. She took the job on this ship because it gave her that opportunity."

"Maybe she decided to stay longer in the area around Naples in order to explore further," Katherine said. "It happens. There's no law requiring passengers and crew to return to a ship."

Sadie shook her head. "No, she wouldn't have done that. She would never quit a job without giving notice and she would never go this long without contacting me."

"I'm sorry," Katherine said. "I wish I could be more helpful."

"You've been helpful just listening to me." Sadie looked around the room and Katherine followed her gaze. Though the rest of the ship was decorated in modern Greek elegance, the Rose Petal boasted floral wallpaper, pastel-colored porcelain and abundant greenery. The effect was of being transported to an English garden—a tribute to Alexandra's English heritage.

"Ariana was the one who encouraged me to take this cruise," Sadie said. "My husband and I spent quite a bit of time in Greece and Italy before we married, but I haven't traveled much since then. This was supposed to be a treat for both of us, traveling together in luxury."

"I'm sorry," Katherine said, feeling the words were inadequate. "Why did you decide to continue, knowing it would be painful traveling without her?"

"I thought coming here might help me find my daughter," Sadie said. She shrugged. "I suppose I read too much detective fiction. The Italian police have assured me they are pursuing every lead, but I can't help thinking that, as her mother, surely, I could do something to help. In any case, at least, here, I feel close to her. I'm hoping I'll learn something that will lead me to her."

The unspoken words *and that she's still alive* hung between them. Katherine's heart hurt, and she pictured her own Gemma in danger. She leaned over and grasped Sadie's hand. "If there's anything I can do to help, let me know," she said. "We all want Ariana to be safe and well."

Sadie nodded and stood. "Thank you. I appreciate that."

She left and Katherine sat alone for a while, enjoying the quiet. Her problems seemed small in comparison to Sadie's. Gemma had spent the summer working on *Alexandra's Dream* and now was happy at school in Oxford. Charles was here with her, alive and healthy. She had a successful career, doing the public relations work she enjoyed. She had so much to be thankful for.

So why was she so restless and on edge?

Her gaze came to rest on the portrait of Alexandra that hung on the wall across from the entrance to the tearoom. The painting had been commissioned by Elias when Alexandra was about the age Katherine was now. Mother and daughter had the same fair English skin and light brown hair, but Alexandra's expression was more serene than Katherine ever felt. Surely, her mother had dealt with the worries and tensions of any wife and mother, but the strain never showed.

"What was your secret, Mother?" Katherine whispered. "How did you and Father stay so close all those years? What would you tell me about my own marriage if you were here now?"

Elias's advice had been simple: He'd ordered this cruise as the cure for the ennui Katherine felt was pulling her and Charles apart. "Time alone together is all you need to find your old feelings for one another," Elias had advised on his last visit to their London flat, where he'd sensed the distance between his daughter and son-in-law and Katherine's growing discontent. He'd offered them the use of his vacation home on a private Greek island, but Ariana's disappearance had postponed that trip.

When Katherine had broken the news that they'd have to cancel their island holiday, she'd searched Charles's eyes for signs of disappointment and, instead, had found only relief. The knowledge that he was as reluctant as she was to spend time alone together—to risk discovering, once and for all, that their marriage was over—saddened her.

The two of them would have put aside the idea of a vacation, altogether, but Elias would not let the notion drop. In the end, he'd booked them on this cruise and presented the holiday as a gift they couldn't refuse.

So here they were, three hours into the cruise and they'd spent less than half an hour together. It didn't say much for their chances of success. If they didn't seek out each other's company on a vacation like this, what did that say about their prospects of spending the rest of their lives together?

Would she and Charles be together to celebrate a sixtieth anniversary, or would they part company long before then, another casualty of real life getting in the way of true love?

CHAPTER TWO

THE EMPIRE ROOM aboard *Alexandra's Dream* featured fine dining in an elegant setting of gold brocade chairs, dazzling white table linens and the finest crystal and china. Katherine saw her mother's tastes reflected everywhere in the room, from the crystal chandeliers overhead, to the plush carpeting beneath her feet. Her father and sister were surely channeling Alexandra's spirit when they chose the decor. Alexandra had been famous for her skill as a hostess. Dinners at her home were always elegant affairs with the finest food and conversation.

Katherine hadn't wanted any preferential treatment on this cruise, and, while she and Charles waited to be shown to a table, June and Albert Westcott entered the dining room. Albert wore a dark suit and carefully knotted tie, while June was resplendent in a silver sequined gown. "How wonderful to see you again," June exclaimed, as if they were long-lost friends.

And, indeed, Katherine thought, it was impossible not to feel as at ease with the older couple as if she'd known them all her life.

"Are you waiting for a table?" June asked. She stood

on tiptoe and looked past them. "There doesn't seem to be a great many tables for two available."

"We should eat together," Charles said. "We'll be seated faster and we can get to know each other better."

Katherine glanced at her husband. Was he merely being his usual congenial self, or was this another way to avoid spending more time alone with her?

"Oh, that would be wonderful!" June exclaimed. She turned to Katherine. "If you're sure we wouldn't be imposing."

"Of course not," Katherine said. It would be rude to deny June when she expressed such obvious pleasure in dining with them. There would be time enough later for her and Charles to be alone.

"Have you been enjoying your cruise so far?" Charles asked after they were seated and their server had taken their drink orders.

"Oh, my, yes!" June leaned forward, eyes shining. "This afternoon we toured the whole ship. I had the most fabulous chocolates in the Temptations café and then we played bingo by the outdoor pool and I won a bottle of wine. Tomorrow morning I have an appointment at the spa. While I'm doing that, Albert is going to try his hand at the driving range. And we've signed up for one of the shore excursions in Kusadasi."

"My, you *have* been busy," Katherine said. She was easily forty years younger than June, yet, she wasn't sure she could have matched the older woman's pace.

"I wish I had your energy," Charles said. "You look as if you're ready to keep going until dawn."

June laughed. "We might do that. After all, at our age, time is precious. I don't want to waste any of it."

Katherine looked away and caught Charles's eye. He smiled, as if sharing a joke with her, though she wasn't sure what it was. Still, the smile went a long way toward improving her mood.

The waiter returned with their drinks and took their dinner orders. "What have you been doing today, dear?" June asked Katherine when the waiter left them.

"I've been enjoying relaxing," she said. When she'd returned to the penthouse after her visit with Sadie Bennett in the tearoom, she'd found Charles engrossed in some work on his laptop. He'd brushed aside her suggestion that they visit the pool, saying he had to answer this e-mail from one of his clients, as it was urgent and couldn't wait until he returned to London.

Katherine wanted to tell him she thought spending time with her ought to be more important than any client, but what would be the use? Instead, she'd taken a magazine onto one of the lounge chairs on the deck. The gentle motion of the ship combined with the warm sun had lulled her to sleep.

She'd awakened almost too late to dress for dinner. Charles, fresh from a shower and looking dashing in his dark gray suit, hadn't understood her irritation at him for letting her sleep.

"Katherine's been working so hard lately, running her business and getting our daughter, Gemma, ready for school, she's overdue for a rest," Charles said now.

"What kind of work do you do?" Albert asked.

"I have my own public relations company," Katherine said.

"Public relations. Now there's a business," Albert said. "June would have been good at something like that. She never met a stranger."

"I find people interesting," June said. "Everyone has a story to tell."

What would her story be, when all was said and done? Katherine wondered. How would she be remembered—dutiful oldest daughter, devoted mother, successful businesswoman? Would her marriage be the only area in her life where she'd failed?

The waiter delivered their meals. Katherine hadn't realized how hungry she was until the snapper Provençal was set in front of her. "This looks delicious," she said.

"I'd like to make a toast." June held her wineglass aloft. "To love and friendship."

"To love and friendship," they echoed, and clinked glasses.

As they ate, June proved true her profession that she enjoyed listening to people's stories. She kept the conversation going with gently probing questions about Katherine's and Charles's lives. By the time the dessert cart arrived, she knew all about Gemma and their flat in London and even their cat, Susie.

"Now, I know you're in public relations," she said, happily diving into a serving of chocolate mousse. "But what do you do for a living, Charles?"

"I'm an architect," Charles said.

"That must be very interesting work," June said. "Do

you design houses or bridges or office buildings—or all of the above?"

"Mostly office buildings and public buildings, though I have designed a few houses."

"Do you know the Trafalgar Bank building in London? The new one?" Katherine asked.

Albert nodded. "Saw a picture of it in the paper."

"That was Charles's design," she said.

"Oh, my, that's wonderful." June beamed. "No wonder she's so proud of you."

Katherine realized she *was* proud of Charles. He'd worked very hard to reach the success he enjoyed today. His designs were known and respected all over the world. She had never begrudged him the time he spent building up his business because she always thought of it as something he did for their family—so that he could provide them with the best kind of lifestyle.

Only, lately, now that she was not so caught up in establishing her own business and, now that Gemma was away from home and not needing her mother every day, Katherine wondered if she'd been *too* accepting of all the time Charles spent away from home. Somehow, she'd expected them to spend more time together at this stage in their lives.

Where was the second honeymoon her friends talked about when their children left for school? Why instead did she feel so empty and so alone?

June pushed aside her empty dish and took a sip of coffee.

"I think fall is the perfect time of year for cruising, don't you?"

"I understand the ports are less crowded this time of year," Charles said. "And the weather is good."

"I'm looking forward to seeing all the wonderful places we'll be visiting," June said. "Rome and Florence. And Monte Carlo! I can hardly sleep for thinking about it." She laughed. "You've probably been to all those places before, but I've never even been away from England."

June's enthusiasm made Katherine see the trip ahead of them in a fresher light. True, she had visited most of the ports on the ship's itinerary at one time or another, but here was her chance to see them with new eyes— not as a businessperson or even a casual tourist, but with the eyes of a lover on a second honeymoon. If she adopted this attitude, surely that would enhance the whole voyage.

"Are you going to see the show in the theater this evening?" June asked. "It's a hypnotist and magician."

I could use a little magic in my life, Katherine thought. She looked at Charles. "Shall we go?"

He nodded. "Why not?"

They left the dining room and made their way up to the theater to a table for four. The entertainer was very good, keeping up a steady patter of jokes and magic tricks. Katherine couldn't remember the last time she'd laughed so much.

Charles was having a good time, too. He looked five years younger when he was relaxed like this. He really did work too hard. She was glad he'd come on this vacation if for no other reason than it provided a bit of a break from his job.

A break they both needed, she reminded herself.

"Now I will need a volunteer from the audience to assist me," the magician announced.

June was out of her seat immediately, waving her arms. "Oh, love, pick me!"

He obliged by asking her to come up. "Have you ever been hypnotized before?" he asked.

"No, love, but I'll try anything once." She winked at the audience, who responded with laughter and applause.

"Are you sure she was never on stage?" Katherine asked Albert.

He smiled and shook his head. "No, but I always said she could have been, if she'd really wanted."

"I'm going to hypnotize you now," the magician said. "You don't need to do anything but relax." He asked June to focus on the pen he held in his hand. As he moved it slowly back and forth in front of her face, he asked her to relax deeper and deeper and deeper...

June slumped in her chair, her body limp, but she was still smiling. Albert leaned forward, gripping the arms of his seat until his knuckles were white. "I'm sure she's fine," Katherine whispered.

"I'm sure you're right." He sat back, though his hold on his seat remained firm. "I'm the worrier in the family."

"Now, June," the magician said. "It's time for tea. And your guest today for tea is none other than the queen herself."

June suddenly came to life. She jumped up from her chair and sketched an elaborate curtsy. "Welcome, Your Majesty," she said. "I'm so honored to have you take tea with me."

She pantomimed pouring tea and lifted her cup to her lips, her pinkie held dramatically in the air. She laughed and made small talk. "I know just what you mean, Your Majesty. My children have been a trial at times, too. But then they've all turned out well in the end, haven't they?"

Albert relaxed, laughing. "Wait till I tell our children about this," he said. "It's so like their mum."

After more tea talk and laughter, the magician put June into a trance once more, then woke her with a snap of his fingers. "How do you feel?" he asked.

"I feel wonderful," she said. "When are we going to start?"

"You've already done your part, June. Thank you very much." He helped her from her chair. "Ladies and gentlemen, a round of applause for my lovely volunteer."

June returned to their table. "What happened?" she asked. "I don't remember a thing."

"You had tea with the queen," Albert said, holding her chair for her. "You were wonderful."

"Was I, really?" She patted his hand. "You'll have to tell me all about it later."

The magician announced that he would make his assistant disappear. A young woman dressed in a sequined leotard joined him on stage. Some time was spent testing the secure nature of the clear glass booth that was wheeled in after her. The young woman entered the booth, the magician waved his wand…and she was gone!

The audience gasped. "Where did she go?" June asked.

"There's probably a trapdoor in the floor or something," Charles said.

"I don't know," June said. "Maybe she really did disappear." She leaned across the table and spoke in a low voice. "I heard there was a young woman who worked on this ship—the librarian—and she disappeared. I wonder if she knew the magician?"

Ariana Bennett again. Katherine shivered. What had happened to her? If she was safe, why didn't she contact someone? Why didn't she contact her mother? And, if she wasn't safe, did her disappearance have any connection to someone on board *Alexandra's Dream?*

The idea was disturbing. Though this cruise line was her father's pet project, in her role overseeing public relations for the line, Katherine had an interest in keeping the ship's reputation pristine. And, as Elias's daughter, she wanted this new project to be a success for him. Refurbishing *Alexandra's Dream* had brought him out of his grief and given him a new focus in life.

If something happened to damage the reputation of the ship, if would be a personal blow to Elias. And a blow to Katherine, as well.

Subject: Smooth Sailing
Date: October 6, 2007
From: Megaera@Netmail.net
To: jacquesw@suissetel.com

I received your e-mail expressing your concerns over the transportation of our goods to America. I disagree that the discovery of certain items on board ship compromises our mission in any way. That was months ago. We are perfectly safe. The artifacts will

arrive stateside as planned. Our two operatives on board the ship will see to their transfer as planned. Everything is in place for our success. The items we are transporting are in great demand in the States and we are assured of a significant profit. Your fears of discovery will seem foolish when you are holding the money in your hand. In the meantime, leave everything to me.
M

THE E-MAIL WAS SENT via a secure connection, one more petty detail seen to. Jacques would be reassured, his greed overcoming his nervousness. Thankfully, *he* was not the one in charge or they would have failed long ago. He served a purpose—to distance the authorities from the real power in their organization—but, when the time came, he would be expendable.

The plan was no less than brilliant. Carefully crafted and executed, the end results would be both riches and revenge. What satisfaction there would be in seeing Elias Stamos not merely damaged, but destroyed, his beloved ship and vaunted reputation in tatters.

But even perfect plans required overcoming complications. The discovery of the smuggled artifacts on board ship had been dealt with and she felt confident it wouldn't happen again. The other items were still safe.

What Jacques did not know—and what she had no intention of telling him or the two operatives aboard ship—was that the items in question would never, in fact, make their way into the hands of the North American buyers. She knew she might have to pay off First Officer Giorgio Tzekas and Mike O'Connor, the fake priest, a little extra to keep them quite, but it would be a small price to pay. When the time was right, a tip would be given to the police in Greece. The ship would be searched and the contraband discovered, with the bill of sales linking them to Elias. He'd be accused of smuggling, arrested even. Reviled as a criminal who had betrayed the country he loved.

An almost sexual heat filled her at the thought. To see the look on Elias's face when the police arrived would be so sweet. A payback for all the pain he'd caused her. The idea had kept her going through all the setbacks.

Ariana Bennett had proved a complication, with her snooping, but she'd been removed from the scene by that other troublemaker, Dante Colangelo. Was he another rival, or working for the police?

It didn't matter. As long as both he and Ariana were kept out of the way until Elias was taken care of. The timeline could be shifted if needed, but they could not be allowed to interfere.

The computer signaled an incoming message and she called it up, expecting a reply from Jacques. Instead, the latest message from the Interpol contact glowed on the laptop screen. The woman was another annoyance and the money she charged for information amounted to extortion. But the plan depended on the intel she provided. And, if the latest message was correct, she'd earned her fee this time, at least.

The two you seek have been located on a private yacht near Capraia. Arrived ten days ago.

CAPRAIA WAS an island in the Tuscan archipelago. No doubt they thought they were safe there. But she couldn't take a chance on them interfering with her plans. They might go to the police, or try to interfere with the smuggling ring that was her ticket to wealth.

Expenses were eating up more and more of the profit every day, and that was one more reason to hurry and get this over with. She did not plan to work for the rest of her life, not when she deserved so much more. Others didn't have to struggle to live in luxury—why should she?

She hit the delete button to erase the e-mail and let out a sigh of frustration. Once again, it was up to her to keep things going. And that meant spending even more money to hire someone to take care of Ariana Bennett and the troublesome Dante.

The idea of dealing with thugs repelled her, but the job required professionals. And she couldn't trust anyone else to make the arrangements. Fortunately, she had resources to call upon.

She opened a desk drawer and depressed a hidden lever. A secret compartment at the back of the drawer opened and, from it, she retrieved a black leather-bound address book. She quickly found the number she was looking for and dialed it.

"*Yahsu?*" A gruff man's voice answered in Greek.

"Where can I find Jiri?"

"Who wants to know?" His tone was guarded.

"Someone who will pay well for a job."

"What kind of job?"

"I have two…friends. Vacationing on a yacht near Capraia. Do you know it?"

"Yes."

"I need someone to visit these two. To take them off the yacht and bring them to Vathi."

"The fishing village."

"That's right. Can you do it?"

"There are only the two of them?"

"That's right. A man and a woman." She hesitated. "The man may be armed." Dante Colangelo did not strike her as a man who went about without a weapon near at hand. He had a certain…lethal look about him. The kind of man she, herself, would have found attractive under other circumstances.

"It will take two of us, then. Myself and a friend." He named a price that was ridiculously high.

"I will give you half of that."

"You will pay all or find someone else."

"Half now, then, and half when you deliver them to Vathi."

"Yes. But, if you try to cheat us, I promise you will not like the consequences."

She shivered, but pushed away the fear. "I will wire the money, along with a description of the two you seek, this afternoon."

"Very good. And who will the message be from?"

She smiled. "You may call me Megaera." A goddess of vengeance whom Elias would be sorry he had ever wronged.

WHILE THE REST OF the passengers enjoyed the magic show, danced in the Polaris Lounge, gambled in the casino or relaxed in their cabins, Sadie retreated to the ship's library. Though the videos, DVDs and more expensive books were locked away at this hour and the young woman who had been hired to take Ariana's place as librarian was not present, cruise passengers were free to use the tables and comfortable chairs as a quiet retreat from the hubbub of the active ship and shelves of inexpensive paperbacks were available on the honor system.

This was the place Sadie felt closest to Ariana. Here was where her daughter had worked, surrounded by the books she loved. And here Sadie hoped to find some clue as to what had happened to the girl.

Her mother's intuition told her that her daughter was still alive and in trouble. Some kind of danger. The two had always been close. Her husband, Derek, Ariana's father, had been away so much, traveling for his job as a museum curator. Sadie and Ariana had become a little team of two. She did her best to include Derek when he was home, but she often wondered if he hadn't felt like an outsider.

As for Ariana, she had worshipped her father. She was never happier than when he was home, and he had shared with her his love of Greek and Roman myths, history and architecture. The two spent hours together poring over books and conversing in the ancient languages that were a puzzle to Sadie.

She remembered one incident, when Ariana was twelve. Sadie had decided Ariana should attend summer camp, where she'd benefit from outdoor activities and make friends with girls her own age. Though she'd been sickly as a small child, Ariana was healthier now. Sadie worried her daughter's bookish ways might lead to a return to ill health later. And she was also concerned that Ariana spent more time with adults and ancient texts than she did with friends her own age.

Ariana balked at the idea of going away to camp, and Derek sided with his daughter. "She can come to work with me this summer," he'd said. "She'll learn more there than she ever will at some silly girls' camp."

"Maybe she'll learn to be a silly girl," had been Sadie's retort. "Doesn't it ever worry you that Ariana is far too serious for a girl her age? She should be giggling over rock singers and exchanging notes with girlfriends instead of spending her days cataloging dusty artifacts and writing in ancient Greek."

"Ariana is no ordinary girl," Derek had said. "She's too smart to waste her time with such foolishness. She's concerning herself with things that are important."

But life outside a museum is important, too, Sadie had thought, but she had kept silent. Derek was proud that Ariana shared his interests. Sadie sometimes wondered if Derek didn't encourage Ariana's fascination with ancient Greek and Rome precisely because it was the only thing in her life that Ariana did not share with her mother. It was something for father and daughter alone, a cord that bound them together in spite of Derek's long absences and lack of involvement in their daily family life.

Derek's arrest on charges of dealing in stolen antiquities had stunned them all. Sadie had visited her husband in prison and realized she didn't really know him anymore. He had another life apart from their little family that she knew nothing about.

Ariana had been fierce in her defense of her father. She was sure evidence would surface to prove his innocence. But Derek's death from a heart attack at age fifty-five had cut that dream short.

Sadie had been stunned and saddened. But she and Derek had been distant both physically and emotionally so long that she couldn't say she felt his absence now too keenly.

Ariana, though, had mourned her father's passing for months. And, though she had never said so out loud, Sadie knew Ariana was determined to prove her father's innocence. She'd told her mother she took the cruiseship job in order to visit the places her father had loved, but Sadie wondered if Ariana was also looking for something that would clear her father's name and allow her to hold on to his memory untarnished.

She first searched the writing desk in the corner, but it held no clues, only stationery with the ship's logo and slips for checking out books.

Next, she turned to the shelves. The library had a selection of books on Greek history and travel—most safely locked away. Sadie would have to return during operating hours to search these. That left the paperbacks, mostly fiction—mysteries, romance, the latest bestsellers. But, at the end of one shelf, Sadie found a small collection of paperback guides to the various regions the ship visited—the kind of guides published by tourist bureaus and chambers of commerce. Perhaps Ariana had looked through these for information about places her father had visited.

Sadie pulled a slim volume from the shelf and examined it for some note in a margin, or an underlined passage that would provide some clue as to her daughter's thoughts and intentions.

Nothing.

With a sigh, she replaced a volume on *Day Trips on the Amalfi Coast* and drew out one titled *Doric Temples of the Magna Grecia.* As she did so, a slip of paper fluttered to the floor. A single word was written on it. *Paestum.* Underlined. Sadie squinted at the handwriting. It might have been Ariana's, but with one word it was difficult to tell.

Paestum. Was it the name of a town? Or a person? She searched the table of contents and the index of the book but found no mention of Paestum.

She set the book aside and turned to a large atlas on a stand in the corner. There she found Paestum. A village on the outskirts of Naples. Near where Ariana had disappeared. Sadie's heart pounded as she stared at the dot on the map. Had Ariana gone to Paestum, or was this note merely a coincidence, having nothing to do with her?

If Ariana *had* visited Paestum, what had she found there? And where was she now?

CHAPTER THREE

To: GMMA@edu.net
From: k_stamos@stamospr.com
Subject: We're on our way

Hi, Gemma,
Just wanted to let you know we set sail without a hitch. It's a different feeling, being on *Alexandra's Dream* as "customers" instead of "employees" but we are enjoying it. This morning we will dock in Kusadasi. I hope to do some sightseeing.

We've met some interesting fellow travelers, in particular, an older couple from London who are celebrating their sixtieth wedding anniversary. June and Albert are so full of fun and life. I know you would love them. Ariana Bennett's mother is here, as well. Poor woman, she is obviously worried sick about Ariana. I can't imagine what happened to make the young woman take off like that without telling anyone. The authorities in Naples have found no sign of foul play and the investigator your grandfather hired hasn't found anything, either.

The gossip on board ship is that she had a fight with

Giorgio Tzekas and left the ship out of embarrassment. Giorgio denies this, but not very strongly. I suspect he enjoys being seen as the kind of man who
would break a young woman's heart.
You knew Ariana better than I did, having spent more
time with her when you were working on the ship this
summer. Why do you think she left? I'd really like to
hear your thoughts.
How is school? Are you enjoying your classes? Don't
stay out too late or eat too much junk food. I know
you're making a face as you read this, but I can't help
being a mom. You know I love you and I miss you.
Hugs, Mom

KATHERINE HIT SEND, then shut down the computer. She
still got a little teary when she thought of her daughter
so far away. Not that Oxford was that far from London,
but, now that Gemma was living away from home,
Katherine was no longer part of her daughter's daily
life. She missed relating the days' events as they cleared
up after tea, or the exchange of confidences over a late-
night cup of cocoa when Gemma returned from a date.

Now Gemma was in a world of her own, studying at
Oxford with the goal of one day realizing her dream of
teaching. She had made new friends that Katherine did
not know and was involved in events and activities
Katherine would never hear about. Never again would
she be as much a part of Gemma's life as she had always
been before now. The knowledge hurt, and Katherine
couldn't help worrying about what could go wrong.

Of course, Gemma was a smart, responsible young

woman and she was quite capable of looking after herself, as she'd proved when she'd worked in the ship's children's center this past summer. But she would always be Katherine's little girl and it was hard letting go of the tether that had bound them so close all these years.

Charles emerged from the bathroom, newspaper in hand. "Did you get your message off to Gemma?" he asked.

"Yes." She shut the laptop and pushed back from the desk. "I hope she's doing okay. She was afraid she wouldn't get all the classes she wanted. And I hope she found that one textbook she needed."

"She'll be fine. You worry too much."

"I didn't say I was worried. I want things to go well for her and I care about what happens to her."

"You worry."

She clamped her mouth shut, biting back an angry retort. She wasn't going to fight on this trip, especially with a man who was so impossible to fight with. Charles was always calm and unperturbed.

"I thought we could disembark at Kusadasi and do some sightseeing," she said. "I hear the ruins at Ephesus are particularly interesting." If nothing else, she ought to be able to lure Charles with the promise of architectural relics.

He shook his head. "I'll pass this time. I need to stay and finish this report for the Malaysian office. You go ahead without me."

She frowned. "I hope you're not going to work the whole trip," she said.

"I won't. I promise. I just need to get this job out of

the way." He patted her shoulder. "You know how it is when you have your own business. There's no one else to put out the fires."

She nodded. She did know. But that didn't make it any easier to accept the distance that had grown between them. Was it their work that pushed them apart, or a growing indifference?

On deck, she joined the throng of passengers disembarking at Kusadasi. Some crowded around guides for organized tours of the ancient ruins of Ephesus. Others, like Katherine, set out on their own through the main part of the city.

As she started across the brick street near the harbor. She heard a man call her name. "Katherine!"

Turning, she saw a tall, handsome man striding toward her and couldn't hold back a smile. "Tom! How good to see you."

Tom Diamantopoulos was chief engineer of *Alexandra's Dream.* When Katherine had briefly joined the cruise earlier in the season, she had shared a few enjoyable dinners with him and Captain Nick Pappas.

She stopped and waited for him to thread his way through the crowds to join her. Tall and tan, dressed in khaki trousers and a short-sleeved peach-colored cotton shirt, he looked more like a professional golfer than part of the crew of a cruise ship. His thick dark hair and perfect features led more than one female to turn and cast an admiring glance his way as he passed.

"You must be off duty this morning," she said.

"Yes. I've never been to Kusadasi before, so I figured I'd see a little of the sights."

"Exactly what I thought."

"Charles isn't with you?" He looked past her, as if expecting to see her husband.

"No, he stayed behind to catch up on some work."

Tom's grin broadened. "Then, you're on your own."

She nodded. Now that Tom was here, the idea of exploring the area held more appeal. "I don't suppose you'd like some company?" she asked.

"I'd like it very much." He swept his arm toward the city stretched out before them. "What would you like to see first?"

"It doesn't matter. It's all new to me."

The depression that had dragged at her that morning lifted beneath the bright sun and Tom's even brighter smile.

They walked into the city and explored the narrow cobbled streets lined with shops and tavernas. Katherine bought a gold bracelet she knew Gemma would like and a pair of earrings for herself. They admired the stained-glass windows and ornate carvings in the Fortress Mosque and marveled at the view of the sea from the town.

When they were both hot and thirsty they stopped in a taverna and ordered shish kebab and bottles of mineral water.

How have you been?" Tom asked, settling in the chair across from her. "You look well."

"I am well," she said. "I've been busy with work, but that's slowed down some and I have more time to myself now that Gemma is away at school."

"I still can't believe you have a daughter old enough to be in college. You must have had her when you were still a child yourself."

She knew he was flirting, but the compliments felt good. At thirty-five, Tom was one of the youngest senior officers on the ship and a favorite with the female staff and passengers. It was easy to see why: Between his Brad Pitt blue eyes and masculine Greek charm, he made every woman he was with feel like the belle of the ball.

"So tell me the latest gossip on board ship," she said when the waiter had set their food in front of them. "Has anything exciting happened lately?"

"Let's see…" He considered the question for a moment, then said, "One of the massage therapists, a young woman from China, apparently hid her baby on board the ship for weeks and only a few people knew about it. From what I understand, her late husband was some kind of human rights activist in China and Lin, the young woman, feared his parents would take the baby from her if they knew about it. Gideon Dayan helped her get away safely and she and the baby are living in Paris now. I think she and Gideon are still seeing each other."

"I had heard something about that," Katherine said. "From my father. But I can see you're the man to come to for all the juicy details," she teased.

He grinned. "You know how it is. A cruise ship is like a floating small town. In such close quarters, you can't help but know everyone else's business."

They devoted themselves to the meal in silence for

a while, then Katherine thought of something else she should ask him. "Have you heard any rumors about Ariana Bennett? Does anyone have any ideas about where she's gone?"

He shrugged. "Nothing new. She was interested in the history of the area and archeology. Someone said she was asking about active digs around Naples—but lots of tourists visit those. You'd think if something had happened to her at one of the digs, someone would have seen her and reported it."

Katherine sighed. "You know her mother, Sadie Bennett, is on the ship this cruise?"

"No, I didn't know that." He drained his bottle of water. "What is she doing here? Does she think she's going to find her daughter when the rest of us have failed?"

"I think she hoped being where her daughter had been so recently might give her some insight," Katherine said. "That, and she was probably going crazy sitting at home doing nothing." She followed the trail of condensation down the side of her glass. "If it was Gemma missing, I'd do the same."

"How is Gemma?" Tom asked, seeming eager to change the subject.

"She's doing great." Katherine couldn't help but smile when she thought of her beautiful, vivacious daughter. "She was really excited about beginning her studies."

"And you miss her terribly."

She glanced at him, surprised by the comment and the sympathy in his voice. "Yes, I do. Does it show so much?"

He smiled. "Only because I feel I know you pretty well. And I saw how the two of you were together."

She nodded, ignoring the flutter in her stomach at his mention of knowing her well. They'd shared a few dinners, some long conversations, some laughter. Not much, but then, how much more time had she and Charles spent together lately?

She pushed back her chair. "I'm tired of sitting." She gathered her purse and her packages and set out walking.

Tom caught up with her. "Did I say something just now to upset you?" he asked.

She shook her head. "Of course not. I'm just anxious to see the rest of the city."

"We could hire a car to take us to Ephesus," he suggested.

She hesitated. Touring ruins without Charles along to explain all the intricacies of the architecture would be a novel experience, indeed. And, it would be his own fault for not accompanying her today. "All right. Turkey is one country I've missed on my travels. I shouldn't pass up the opportunity to explore it now."

A driver was quickly located who agreed to take them the thirty kilometers to Selcuk, site of the Ephesian ruins. Once there, they decided against hiring a guide in favor of exploring the area on their own with the help of a guidebook Tom bought from a pretty young vendor, who blushed and fluttered under the attentions of the handsome ship's officer.

"I think if you'd suggested it, she would have left her stall to follow you," Katherine teased.

Tom shrugged. "What can I say? Women like me." His eyes met hers, his expression warm. "I'm more particular about who I take a real interest in, however."

She looked away, not sure if she should feel flattered by this admission or not. Tom seemed to be saying *she* was a woman who held his particular interest, but why? She was a married woman, not free to be anything more than a casual friend.

Unless he was trying to tell her he had no scruples about being more than a friend to her *in spite of* her marriage to Charles.

She pushed the idea aside and tried to focus her attention on the pillars of the Basilica of St. John that Tom was pointing out to her.

They walked without talking for a while, past airy white marble temples and museums celebrating every aspect of ancient Ephesian culture and geography. Katherine pretended interest in the sites, but most of her awareness was on the man at her side. She found herself unconsciously matching her steps to his and studying the way his shadow overlapped hers. With each breath she caught the faint, spicy of his cologne. Here on this dusty street, surrounded by dozens of other people, the cries of seabirds and the blare of honking horns and the calls of vendors adding to the chaotic scene, she was more conscious of being a woman than she had been in years.

She stumbled over a rough place in the pavement and Tom put his hand at her back to steady her and kept it there. The heat of his touch seeped into her, warming places that she was not even aware had been cold.

DANTE COLANGELO had built a successful career on his ability to judge people and their motives. The judgment had helped him survive many a dangerous situation and allowed him to rise to the level of investigator in the *Guardia de Finanza* at a young age.

But he found himself continually questioning his judgment when it came to the beautiful American, Ariana Bennett. He watched her now out of the corner of his eye as she reclined in one of the deck chairs in the stern of the yacht, intent on the screen of her iPod. What was it about the electronic device that was so fascinating?

Or was this merely her attempt to ignore him?

He could not blame her for her distrust of him. She knew him only in his role as part of the organized-crime group that had taken over the dig site she'd visited outside of Naples.

He could not risk blowing his cover by revealing his true identity, nor was he entirely convinced of her innocence. She had admitted to visiting the dig site to learn more about her late father's connection to the area, but was she really ignorant of Derek Bennett's role in the smuggling ring—or was she merely getting a feel for the operation before she demanded her share of the proceeds as her father's daughter?

Unwilling to stand by and watch her ruin months of investigative work, either through her meddling or her ignorance, he'd had no choice but to kidnap her and take her away from the dig site.

She glanced up and saw him watching her, and he

quickly looked away, but not before he recognized the anger burning in her eyes.

The anger stung, but he pushed aside the hurt. He could not let sentiment, or a beautiful, seemingly vulnerable woman, distract him from his duty.

He stared out over the side of the ship, at the sparkling waves and the rocky coastline of Capraia. From here the sole village on the tiny island looked like the postcards sold to tourists. Picturesque and harmless. Only a man like him knew the crime even such quiet places could harbor. The branch of the Camorra he was investigating was taking over dig sites throughout Italy, literally stripping the country of its heritage and pocketing a fortune in illegal profits in the process.

He looked toward the bow of the boat, and caught a flash of brown in the distance. His stomach tensed as a flicker of memory brightened to a flame. He brought the binoculars to his eyes and pretended to scan the sky for birds, then gradually lowered the glasses until the brown color sharpened to the outline of a boat, a dilapidated craft painted a peculiar shade of yellow-brown, the name on the bow faded to indecipherable hieroglyphics.

A boat he had not seen before, he was sure of it. As he kept the glasses trained on it, a man came up on deck. A bulky man in a gray fisherman's sweater who did not move like any fisherman Dante had ever met. And though, at this distance, he could not be sure, he would have bet the bulkiness under the man's left arm was due to a pistol of some kind in a shoulder holster.

"Sebastian!" he called to the yacht's skipper, a fellow

police officer, who lounged on a high stool in the vessel's cabin.

Sebastian started and jumped to his feet. He raised his hand as if to salute, then remembered himself and assumed a more sullen expression. "What is it?" he asked.

Dante glanced at Ariana. She was still focused on her iPod, but the tension in her shoulders and her stillness told him she was listening. He moved closer to Sebastian and spoke in a low voice. "Start the engines and move us around to the south," he said. "I suspect we have unwelcome visitors."

The lines around Sebastian's mouth tightened. "Camorra?"

Dante nodded. "I believe so. They must have followed us."

Sebastian turned the key in the ignition and the boat roared to life. "Should we try to outrun them?" he asked.

Dante shook his head. "No. It would be too dangerous. See if you can maneuver up into those rocky coves away from town. I will get the girl and slip off the ship, then you can lure our friends away."

Sebastian nodded and Dante left the cabin to talk to Ariana.

She met him just outside the door. "What's going on?" she asked. "Where are we going?"

"We are going ashore," he said in English. He leaned against the rail, a casual pose, though he watched the brown ship out of the corner of his eye. As he had expected, as soon as Sebastian turned their boat away from shore, the brown ship's engines sprang to life, as well. He felt the Glock resting securely in the shoulder holster beneath his jacket. He hoped he would not need to use it, but knowing the Camorra thugs were well armed, he was glad he was not defenseless.

"If we're going ashore, why are we moving away from the town?" Ariana looked back at the town of Capraia, which they were quickly leaving behind.

"We are going to go ashore in a little cove over here," he said.

She looked at him as if he had lost his mind. "No," she said, folding her arms across her chest.

He fixed his gaze fully on her, forcing himself to look stern, to not be distracted by the fear in her blue eyes. "You do not have a choice," he said. "You are going to go ashore with me."

"No."

Amazed, he stared as she sat down on the deck, long legs folded gracefully beneath her, arms still crossed. She stared up at him, her words that of a spoiled child, her expression that of a determined woman. "I won't go."

He curled one hand into a fist, though what he wanted most was to pull her to him and kiss that stubborn expression off her face. "I have a gun," he reminded her. "I could shoot you."

"You won't do that."

She was right of course.

He squatted down until his eyes were almost level with hers. "Do you see that boat behind us?" he asked.

She glanced over her shoulder. "What boat? There are lots of boats out there."

"There is only one following us. The brown one."

Twin lines formed on her forehead as she searched for and found the brown vessel. "It looks like an ordinary fishing boat."

"It does not have an ordinary crew. Until I can determine who they are and what they want, you and I are going to hide out."

Her eyes met his again, and he recognized a glimmer of fear. "Where are we going to hide?" she asked.

"There are caves in those rocks over there beneath the cliffs. If we can get to them, we should be safe."

She followed his gaze toward the cliffs. Waves crashed against jagged rocks, sending up sheets of spray. She wet her lips. "How will we get to these caves?" she asked.

"When I tell you, we will slip off the stern. There is a ladder that leads into the water. From there we can make our way to the caves."

Her skin had bleached the color of Italian marble. "We're going in the water?"

"It is not deep," he said. "We should be able to wade most of the way."

She shook her head. "I can't."

"This is as far as I can go." Sebastian stuck his head out the cabin. "It gets shallow very quickly from here."

"I can't do it," Ariana said again, her voice breathy.

Dante frowned, impatient. "Do you want me to leave you here for those thugs to find?" He leaned closer, deliberately making his voice harsh, his words cruel. "Do you know what men like that do to women like you?"

Her eyes widened and her nostrils flared. This close he could have counted every lacy lash, and the soft scent of her perfume sent inappropriate desire slashing through him.

Impatience changed to admiration as she stood and walked over to the side. Her knuckles whitened as she gripped the rail and her voice was reed-thin when she spoke. "What do I have to do?" she asked.

CHAPTER FOUR

"HELLO, KATHERINE!"

Katherine blinked, pulled from her dangerous fantasies about Tom by the sight and sound of June Westcott hurrying toward her across a crowded plaza. Dressed in orange capris, a yellow-and-orange top and a yellow head scarf, June rivaled the sun for brightness. Albert followed at a more leisurely pace. He wore a camera around his neck and carried shopping bags in each hand.

"Hello," Albert said, and looked inquiringly at Tom.

"June and Albert Westcott, this is Chief Engineer Tom Diamantopoulos. From *Alexandra's Dream,*" Katherine added, fighting back a blush. There was no reason she should feel guilty about walking with a friend.

A friend who just happened to be a handsome man to whom she was attracted. That merely proved she was a healthy, normal woman. There was nothing wrong with a little harmless flirtation and pleasant temptation.

"Where is Charles?" June asked.

"He had to stay behind and finish up some work," Katherine said, annoyed at the fresh stab of guilt the question brought forth. "Have you been enjoying Kusadasi?" she asked. "It looks as if you've done a lot of shopping."

"We've bought the most wonderful souvenirs for the grandchildren and an embroidered dress my daughter will love," June said. "Oh, and a handwoven mat for our neighbor, who is looking after our cat, and some local wine." June laughed. "It's a good thing I brought along an extra suitcase to pack my gifts."

"Why don't you let me carry those back to the ship for you?" Tom asked, relieving Albert of his bags. The old dear did look relieved to be rid of the burden, though he made a feeble protest before surrendering the bags.

"That's very kind of you," June said. "We are a little tired and should go back and rest up."

Tom found a cab that would take the four of them to the dock at Kusadasi. On the drive, June chattered on about the sights they'd seen that day. Katherine was glad that she didn't need to contribute much more to the conversation than an occasional nod. She was feeling worn-out herself, as if she'd wrestled with a tiger.

Not a tiger, she amended, but her own conflicted feelings. She'd enjoyed her morning with Tom, enjoyed the open appreciation in his eyes and the attention he paid her every word. She'd enjoyed the physical awareness and the frank sexual energy between them.

If only she could say she'd enjoyed those things with her husband, instead of a handsome, single man.

While Tom was unloading June's purchases from the cab, Katherine made idle conversation with Albert about the wonders of Kusadasi and the sights they had explored that afternoon. A commotion at a vendor's stall nearby distracted them both. Katherine stared as she recognized Sadie Bennett arguing with a local man.

"Is that someone from our ship?" Tom asked, coming to stand beside Katherine.

She nodded. "It's Ariana Bennett's mother. We'd better see what's going on."

Sadie was so involved in her discussion with the vendor she didn't even notice when Tom and Katherine arrived at her side. The vendor was speaking in a torrent of rapid Turkish, both his hands and his voice raised. Sadie repeatedly attempted to interrupt him, thrusting one of the amulets he sold at him, agitated to the point of tears.

Tom gently touched her elbow. "Mrs. Bennett?" he asked. "Is something wrong?"

Sadie looked at him and shrank back. Then she saw Katherine. "Katherine, thank God you're here. Do you speak Turkish?"

"No," she answered. "But most of the vendors I've met speak a little English."

"Which they conveniently forget whenever there's trouble," Tom said. "Maybe I can help."

"You know Turkish?" Katherine asked, surprised.

"I dated a Turkish girl for a while and she taught me a few things."

And how much of what she taught you would be useful in this situation? she wondered.

Tom turned to Sadie. "What's wrong?"

"I was on my way back to the ship when I saw these amulets." She showed him a small carved figure on a leather thong. "Ariana sent me one not long before she disappeared. It's the Egyptian goddess Tawaret, protector of women and children." She stroked her thumb along the tiny figure which was part hippo, part lion and part crocodile. "I've been trying to ask this man if he remembers selling one to her, but, when I showed him her picture, he became more and more upset." She opened her other hand to show a small photo of a smiling Ariana Bennett.

Katherine felt a rush of sympathy for the grieving woman. She gave Sadie's shoulder a comforting squeeze while Tom addressed the vendor, who had finally grown silent. A brief exchange revealed the problem. "He thinks you're accusing him of trying to cheat your daughter," Tom said.

"No doubt it's happened before," he added. He picked up one of the amulets and examined it. "I doubt this is real, though it's made to look old and some tourists no doubt assume it's authentic—a misconception I doubt he bothers to correct. The shouting is probably an act to prevent him having to pay a refund."

The man scowled at Tom, but said nothing.

"She only wants to know if he remembers selling an amulet like this to her daughter," Katherine said. "She has no complaints about the amulet itself."

Tom relayed this information and the vendor relaxed enough to examine the photo of Ariana. Then he shrugged and mumbled something.

"What did he say?" Sadie asked.

"He says he doesn't remember every tourist who stops here," Tom answered.

Sadie's shoulders slumped. She replaced the photo

in her purse. "I know it was a long shot, but when I saw the amulets, they made me think of her," she said.

Katherine had no doubt almost everything made Sadie think of her missing daughter. She put her arm around the woman and steered her away from the booth. "Come back to the ship with us. You look exhausted."

Sadie nodded and let them lead her to where June and Albert waited a short distance away. By the time the five of them returned to the ship, she was in better spirits. "Thank you for coming to my rescue back there," she said. "I was afraid the vendor was accusing me of stealing the necklace."

"I'm glad we could help." Katherine wanted so much to do something to help Sadie, to ease the burden of grief she must be feeling. "Will you have dinner with us tonight?" she asked.

Sadie nodded. "That would be nice. Thank you. Now I think I'll go to my cabin and lie down for a while."

Katherine returned to her suite. Charles wasn't there. There was no reason he should be, really, but his absence only added to her dark mood. The whole point of this vacation was to spend more time together, but so far they'd done very little of that.

A knock on the door interrupted her brooding. When she opened it, she was startled to see Tom. "I won't keep you," he said. "I just wanted to see how you were doing. You seemed upset when we parted."

She'd thought she'd kept her feelings disguised. How was it that this man she hardly knew had read her emotions so well? "Come in," she said, opening the door wider.

He stepped inside. He'd already changed into his

uniform, the white of his shirt emphasizing his deep tan and blue eyes. Those eyes were filled with concern for her now. "Are you all right?" he asked again.

She nodded. "I was worried about Sadie Bennett." She shrugged. "As a mother myself, I can so easily put myself in her shoes."

"If you like, I'll question Giorgio again about what happened with him and Ariana. Maybe this time he'll tell me something that will help us."

"Would you? I'm still not convinced he had anything to do with her disappearance, but it could help to talk to him."

"Of course. I'll let you know what I find out."

The door to the suite opened and Charles stepped in. He stared at Tom, startled. "Hello?" he said.

"Charles, this is Tom Diamantopoulos, the chief engineer." Katherine hurried to introduce them, hoping Charles wouldn't notice the heightened color in her cheeks. Though why she should blush was beyond her. The two of them had only been talking.

Charles shook Tom's hand. "I ran into Katherine in Kusadasi," Tom explained. "I wanted to make sure she was all right now."

"Why wouldn't she be all right?" Charles asked. Frowning, he turned to Katherine.

"When Tom left me, I was with Sadie Bennett," Katherine said. "She was upset and arguing with a vendor."

Charles still looked confused. Tom moved toward the door. "I'd better go," he said. He nodded to Charles. "Good to meet you."

When they were alone, Charles walked past Katherine and sat on the bed. "What's this about Sadie Bennett?" he asked.

Katherine came and sat beside him. "She was arguing with a vendor, obviously very distraught. She was showing him a picture of her daughter, asking if he remembered her."

"Why would a vendor who sees thousands of tourists every week remember one American woman?" Charles asked.

Katherine shook her head. "I think Sadie is just desperate. I wish I could do something to help."

Charles patted her arm. "You can't mother the whole world, you know? Mrs. Bennett will be all right."

She bristled at his admonition. Is that how Charles saw her—as a mother, not a lover?

And, if he did, was there even any point in trying to change his mind?

THAT NIGHT AT DINNER, Sadie was in a better mood, while Katherine was feeling worse. She picked at her food while Sadie and Charles discussed ancient Greek architecture, a subject Sadie's late husband had had an interest in.

"What did your husband do?" Charles asked.

"He was a museum curator in Philadelphia. His specialty was Greco-Roman antiquities, but his real interest was Greek and Roman mythology and history. I often thought if he hadn't been a curator, he would have made a good professor."

After dinner, Charles suggested a stroll on deck, but Sadie pleaded weariness and left them. Katherine didn't know whether she dreaded being alone with Charles or looked forward to it. Her feelings were so mixed up these days. On one hand, she clung to the hope of re-capturing the closeness they'd once known, on the other she feared those feelings were gone forever.

They were on their way out of the dining room when June stopped them. "You're just the two I'm looking for," she said.

"What can we do for you?" Katherine asked, forc-ing a smile.

"We need you for tonight's entertainment." June took her hand and tugged her toward the Polaris Lounge.

"Oh, I don't know." Katherine hung back. She defi-nitely didn't share June's penchant for being the center of attention.

"It will be fun, I promise," June said. "Please?"

"Why not?" Charles surprised Katherine by siding with June. He smiled. "We're on vacation. Why not try something different?"

So that was how Katherine found herself seated in a chair onstage with June and three other women while Charles waited backstage with the other women's hus-bands. The evening's entertainment was billed as "The Not-So-Newlywed Game." The emcee would ask the women questions about their husbands, then the hus-bands would come out and give their answers. The couple whose answers most closely matched won that round. Then the men would have their turn.

Katherine fidgeted in her chair, sensing a disaster in the making.

The first question was easy. "What is your husband's

favorite color?" Charles always favored blue shirts, so Katherine was pretty sure of that answer.

From there the questions got more difficult. "What is your husband's current favorite singer?"

"What's the name of his hairdresser-barber?"

"Who is his favorite author?"

Katherine floundered, unsure of any of the answers. She felt she should know these things, and was horrified to learn how ignorant she was of the man who lay beside her in bed each night.

When Charles joined her onstage, she could hardly look at him. She knew she had failed to answer most of the questions correctly. What did it say that, after nineteen years of marriage, she knew so little about him?

If Charles was upset at her lack of knowledge of his likes and dislikes, he didn't show it. June won the first round hands down. "The questions were easy because Albert and I listen to the same singers and read the same books," she said, beaming. "We've always had a lot in common. I think that's why we've been so happy all these years."

If that was the criteria for a happy marriage, Katherine thought, she and Charles were doomed.

Then it was time for the men to answer questions about the women. Katherine waited nervously backstage, making small talk with the other women. When she returned to the stage Charles greeted her with a smile and a kiss on the cheek—a surprising show of affection from a normally reserved man.

"All right, ladies, now it's your turn to see how well

your husbands know you," the emcee said. He glanced at the card in his hand. "The first question was 'What is your wife's favorite perfume?'"

"Beyond Paradise," Charles said without hesitation.

Katherine started and looked at him. "That's right." Gemma had given her the scent for Christmas. How had Charles remembered that?

Favorite singer, Dido; favorite movie, *An Affair to Remember;* name of her childhood pet, Winston— Charles answered every question correctly. Katherine stared at him, amazed.

In the end, the contest was decided by a tiebreaker question, which June and Albert won. Katherine didn't blame Charles for not knowing the name of her favorite place to shop—as far as she knew, she didn't have a single favorite.

The realization that Charles knew so much about her—that he had obviously been paying more attention than she had all this time, confused her. If he really was so in sync with her, why didn't she feel it? Was it true caring on his part, or merely his architect's habit of paying attention to details?

"How did you know all those things about me?" she asked as they left the lounge.

"You're my wife." He squeezed her hand. "I ought to have learned a few things about you after all these years."

"I only got one answer right about you," she pointed out.

"You've been busy with Gemma. And the questions they asked the wives were harder." He put his arm around her. "Let's take that walk now," he said. "The moon is out."

She nodded, and let him lead her onto the deck, where they joined other couples strolling along the rail. The moon was a silver disk in a blue-black sky and the waves sparkled with an eerie fluorescence. The scene was wildly romantic, but she was afraid to surrender to it. It would be easy to play the part of life-long lovers in this setting but she needed more assurance there was any real depth to their emotions—that the warmth she felt toward Charles at this moment wasn't just a product of the setting, but born of true, mutual feeling.

"Charles, do you love me?" she asked.

His step faltered. He stopped and stared at her. "What kind of a question is that?"

And what kind of an answer is that? "Do you love me?" she repeated.

"Of course I do. You're my wife." He took her hand and they continued walking.

"One doesn't necessarily follow the other," she said.

"In this case, it does." She waited for him to elaborate, but he did not. Charles had never been a man to waste words, but, tonight, she needed more from him. She wanted to know what he was thinking and why he felt the way he did.

"I don't feel we're as close as we used to be," she said, determined to forge ahead, no matter how painful.

"No one can remain newlyweds forever."

"I'd hoped this trip would be something of a second

honeymoon for us," she said. "A chance to reconnect, away from work and the demands of family."

He glanced at her. "And I agreed. Isn't that what we're doing now? I'm enjoying being with you now. I always enjoy being with you."

How could she explain to him that his physical presence wasn't enough? She wanted to feel the emotional connection they had once shared. She squeezed his hand. "I want us to be close again," she said. "To talk about our hopes and dreams. Our feelings."

He frowned. "I'm not interested in psychoanalyzing our marriage."

"I'm not talking about psychoanalysis. I only want us to talk to each other more. To really communicate."

"I thought that was what we were doing right now."

They were talking, all right, but she doubted they were communicating. She glared at him, searching for something to say that would get through to him—without resulting in an argument.

He slipped his arm around her and pulled her close. "Let's not overthink this. Let's relax and enjoy ourselves. The rest will come."

She wanted to believe him, to have his faith that things would work themselves out, without any effort on their part. But her confidence in that approach had faded. After all, she'd been waiting for their old closeness to return, to flow back in like the tide.

She wasn't sure waiting was enough, anymore. She wanted to *do* something to fix their marriage, but that took Charles's cooperation. Something she wasn't sure he was willing to give.

So where did that leave her—walking arm in arm with a man she loved, but wasn't sure she really knew anymore.

CHARLES ENJOYED WATCHING Katherine when she wasn't aware he was studying her. She was preoccupied tonight, upset by that silly game. Those worries would recede soon enough, replaced by some other concern. In the meantime, he'd wait for her to return to normal and enjoy watching her.

She had a natural grace and was completely unself-conscious. The years had ripened the slender girl he'd married into an attractive woman, one who still aroused a desire whose strength surprised him.

He remembered the first time he'd laid eyes on her. He'd been walking across the beach where he was vacationing with friends in Glyfada, outside Athens, and had noticed a girl sitting at a table near the pier. She was with a group of friends and had thrown her head back and was laughing. He had stopped in his tracks, mesmerized by the sight of her, hair the color of caramel flowing down her back, her skin like rose-tinted porcelain. He'd had trouble breathing for a moment and had found himself walking directly toward her, determined not only to meet her, but to make her his.

Nothing could have been more surprising for a man whose life before that moment had been ruled by logic and order. He'd been drawn to the field of architecture precisely because it was a discipline of line and geometry and solid design principles. Yet, here he was now, acting purely on instinct, already believing himself half in love with a girl he'd seen for the first time scarcely a minute before.

None of this showed in his manner as he approached her, though. He'd merely walked up and stuck out his hand. "Hello, I'm Charles Slater. I saw you just now and had to stop and introduce myself."

She'd looked amused, but had taken his hand and held it in hers. She spoke in a low voice, in slightly accented English. "Hello, Charles, my name is Katherine Stamos."

And that had been that. Her other friends had gradually drifted away, shut out of the conversation by Charles and Katherine's complete focus on one another. They had spent that whole afternoon together, into the evening and had met again the following night. By their third day together, he knew he was going to marry her. By the end of the week, he had proposed, and, while she had not accepted outright, she had agreed to stay in touch and to see more of him.

He'd arranged an internship in his firm's Greek branch in order to be near her and had persuaded her to travel to London with him for a fall holiday. With the single-mindedness of young lovers, they had arranged their whole lives around stolen opportunities to spend a few uninterrupted hours together, laughing, making love and talking about everything under the sun.

Her father, Elias, had not approved of the match, though her mother, Alexandra, had been more gracious. He suspected the fact that he, like Alexandra, was English, had helped his suit with her, though this did little to endear him to Elias. Charles suspected even Alexander the Great or some other Greek hero would not have been deemed good enough for the great man's eldest daughter.

Charles was not poor and he came from a good family, but he was far below the social spheres in which the Stamoses orbited. Elias himself was viewed with almost godlike reverence by his fellow countrymen, known for his devotion to preserving Greek culture and heritage and his generosity toward many worthy causes.

None of which meant anything to Charles, who refused to be cowed. He was prepared to run away with Katherine and elope if necessary. He didn't need the approval of Elias or anyone else in order to build the life he wanted.

In the end, though, the twin efforts of both Katherine and Alexandra had worn down Elias's resistance and he had permitted the marriage to take place. The birth of his first grandchild a year later had led to a thawing of the chill between the two men, and now, eighteen years later, Elias had become one of Charles's champions.

Though this cruise had been presented as a gift from Elias, Charles knew it was an attempt by his father-in-law to repair what he saw as a rift in his daughter's marriage. If not for a reluctance to upset Katherine and Gemma, Charles would have refused the present. Nothing was wrong with his marriage that time would not cure. Ups and downs were normal in any relationship. He and Katherine were in a period of their lives when other demands took time away from their relationship.

The old closeness would return soon enough, he was

sure of it. In the meantime, there was no need to fret. While they were here, they'd take advantage of the opportunity to relax and enjoy themselves.

After all, he and Katherine were meant to be together. Nothing could change that.

DANTE TOOK ARIANA'S ARM and guided her to the stern. "I'll go in the water first," he said, wishing his English was better. If she understood Italian, he was sure he could find the words to reassure her. "You follow me. I will be right there to catch you."

"I...I can't swim," she said, her voice trembling.

He squeezed her arm. "I promise I will not let you go."

And he would do everything in his power to protect her, from the Camorra as well as from the water. His words had been a test as well as a threat. If she was truly afraid of the mob, it added to the evidence that she was not one of them.

He slipped into the water quickly, the cabin and profile of the yacht hiding him from view. The water was up to his chest here, the rough waves making it difficult to hold himself steady.

He widened his stance and put one hand on the ladder to steady himself and reached the other up to her. "Climb down slowly," he said. "I will assist you."

She was so pale, he feared she might faint. He only prayed he would catch her before she hit her head or drowned. She gripped the top of the ladder and froze.

"They're getting closer," Sebastian said.

She glanced back toward the boat, though the cabin

blocked her view, then looked at Dante again. He held both arms up to her. "I will not let you fall," he said. "But we must hurry."

She nodded, then closed her eyes and felt for the first rung of the narrow aluminum ladder. Two steps and he could reach around her, steadying her.

She sagged against him, trembling, and he tightened his hold on her, swallowing past the emotion that knotted in his throat. Her fear and her courage in facing it moved him beyond anything else in memory. He tried to tell himself it was the adrenaline of the moment, or some normal protective instinct of a man for a woman.

But he suspected his feelings for Ariana were rooted in something much deeper, something duty and responsibility made it impossible to examine too closely.

She stretched her foot down toward the next-to-last rung of the ladder just as a large wave slapped the side of the boat and set it to rocking. With a muffled scream, Ariana lost her balance and fell backward.

Dante caught her, his arms encircling her and pulling her close, his heart racing as he cradled her to him. "You are all right," he murmured, stroking her silk-soft hair, allowing himself the luxury of holding her a moment too long for propriety.

She cradled her head on his shoulder, clinging to him, her voice muffled in the leather of his jacket as she spoke. "I can't do this," she whispered.

"You do not have to," he said. Crouching slightly, he slid one arm beneath her knees and hoisted her into his arms. "Hold on tightly," he said. "You will be safe soon."

It was slow going in the choppy water. Slipping and

stumbling but somehow never falling, Dante moved as quickly as possible to the shelter of the caves beneath the cliffs. Ariana kept her face pressed into his jacket, her arms tight around his neck, her body so warm and soft against his.

They reached the entrance to the closest cave, and he waded up onto the narrow sandbar at its mouth and reluctantly set her down. She remained clinging to him for a moment, then pushed away, seemingly reluctant to break the contact, also.

"Thank you," she whispered, not looking at him, smoothing her shirt down over her pants.

"We should be all right now," he said. "But we should probably move deeper into the cave before they see us." He turned to check the position of their pursuers. White light blinded him and the physical force of an explosion knocked him onto his back. He heard screaming and felt a searing pain in his head, rocks and debris raining around him as he slipped into blackness.

CHAPTER FIVE

SADIE WRAPPED HER HAND around the amulet she wore
and said a silent prayer for Ariana's safety. In the let-
ter that had accompanied the amulet, Ariana had explained that the ugly little goddess, Tawaret, was the
protector of mothers and children, but was also a
fierce defender of all women. She wished Ariana had
the amulet with her now, and whatever protection it
might provide.

Sadie had awakened early this morning from a terrible dream, in which her daughter was calling to her,
pleading for help. Now, hours later, that sense of dread
lingered still. Every nerve felt rubbed raw.

As soon as she thought it reasonable to expect the
other passengers to be up and about, she went in search
of Katherine. She found her eating breakfast at the
Garden Terrace buffet. Her husband was with her and
Sadie hesitated to interrupt, but Katherine saw her and
waved her over.

"How are you this morning?" Katherine asked with
obvious concern.

"I didn't sleep well," Sadie admitted.

"I'm sorry to hear that," Katherine said. "Though it's

understandable. Perhaps the ship's doctor could prescribe something to help you sleep."

Sadie shook her head. "That's all right. I'll be fine. I really stopped by to apologize for my behavior yesterday. I wasn't thinking clearly and I appreciate your help." She glanced at Charles. "I got into an argument with a vendor who spoke only Turkish and I speak only English. Katherine and the ship's engineer came to my rescue."

"One has to be careful dealing with these vendors." Charles laid aside his napkin and stood. "If you ladies will excuse me, I promised Albert I'd meet him at the driving range. I have a feeling he's going to beat me badly."

When Charles had left, Katherine gestured to his empty chair. "Won't you join me? There's still tea left, or you could order coffee."

"Thank you. Coffee would be nice." She sat and a waiter rushed over to fill her cup.

"I had an e-mail from my daughter, Gemma, this morning," Katherine said. "She worked on the ship this summer and became friends with your daughter. I asked her about Ariana's mood and what Gemma thought might have happened to her. She said Ariana was definitely not involved with Giorgio Tzokas —that she had rejected all his advances. And she said Ariana seemed excited about visiting the places her father had talked about."

Sadie pleated the edge of the doily beneath her plate, then looked Katherine in the eye. "I didn't tell you the entire truth about my husband the other day in the tearoom," she said. "Shortly before he died, he was arrested and charged with dealing in stolen antiquities.

The accusation shocked us both, but Ariana was particularly devastated."

"I'm so sorry," Katherine said. "That must have been awful."

Sadie nodded. "It was." She could scarcely remember those dark days, the pain so terrible she had blocked it out. "The strain was too much for Derek. He had a heart attack while he was awaiting trial. Ariana blamed the authorities. They didn't endear themselves to either of us when they descended on the house before he was even buried and searched everywhere for evidence against him."

"Hadn't they searched the house when he was first arrested?" Katherine asked.

"Yes, but apparently they felt they hadn't found everything. They returned and went through everything again." She shuddered. "It was like being...violated."

"I can't even imagine how devastating that would be."

Sadie nodded. "I know my husband was no saint. I suspected for some time there were other women in his life. And there was money I couldn't explain—when Ariana was a child, she was quite ill. I was worried sick how we'd afford her treatment. Derek was worried, too—and then all of a sudden, the money appeared. He said he'd gotten a raise, but I always wondered..." She shook her head. "None of that really matters, except that Ariana was crushed by the accusations against her father. To her, he *was* a saint. Or a Greek god." She smiled, remembering how Ariana had preferred the ancient myths of gods and goddesses to ordinary bedtime stories. She would listen for hours as her father wove fantastic tales of those days.

"It's only natural for girls to feel that way about

their father," Katherine said. "Gemma idolizes Charles that way, too."

Sadie's expression sobered. "If Ariana was excited about visiting the places Derek loved, I'm afraid she might also have been trying to find evidence to prove he was innocent. What if she uncovered something she wasn't supposed to? Something that put her life in danger?"

Katherine gripped her hand. "You mustn't think that way."

"I had a dream last night. A nightmare, really. Ariana was in danger and calling for help."

"Anxiety produces those kinds of dreams. It doesn't mean they're true."

Sadie stood. "I've decided it's time to go to the press. Tell our story to the newspapers and let them publicize it."

Katherine's eyes widened. "Are you sure that's wise? My father has already made inquiries—"

"And he's learned nothing. If we publicize Ariana's disappearance, put out bulletins and posters, we're more likely to find someone who saw her. Someone who knows something."

Katherine pressed her lips together. "Going to the media might also alert anyone involved with Ariana's disappearance. It might even lead them to harm her."

Sadie took a deep breath. She hadn't thought of that, but what other choice did she have? "I have to do something," she said. "I can't bear to sit here idle, any longer."

"Before you go to the press, talk to my father," Katherine said. "He may have ideas we haven't explored yet."

Sadie hesitated. She hated to waste any more time,

when Ariana might truly need her. But Elias Stamos had been very kind to her before. "All right." She nodded. "Please ask your father to contact me. But I don't want to wait too long."

"I'll get in touch with him right away." Katherine pushed back her chair and stood, also.

Sadie left the restaurant, the amulet heavy between her breasts. She would talk to Elias. But not even he could stop her from doing everything possible to find her daughter.

KATHERINE SENT an urgent e-mail to her father. She told him Sadie Bennett wanted to take the story of Ariana's disappearance to the press.

I've convinced her to wait and talk to you, first, but she's very determined. Would it be possible for you to meet with both of us in Naples when the ship docks there? Together, perhaps we'll be able to persuade her that involving the media is not a good idea.

SADIE SEEMED to hold Elias in high regard. Katherine only hoped her father could sway the woman away from this idea of bringing in the media. Yes, the press would give a lot of publicity to Ariana's disappearance—exactly the sort of publicity a newly launched cruise line did not need. If people thought *Alexandra's Dream* wasn't safe, they would cancel bookings and take their business elsewhere.

If the cruise line failed, Katherine had no doubt her father's disappointment would be keen. This project was special to him, related as it was to the memory of his wife. As the representative of both the family and the company on board, Katherine felt responsible. Most of all, she hated the idea of letting her father down. And, as much as she felt for Sadie, she was convinced that going to the press would not bring her any closer to finding Ariana.

Unfortunately, all she could do now was wait and hope that Sadie would keep her promise not to take her story to the press until she'd spoken with Elias.

This, the third day of the cruise, was a day at sea, a day for the passengers to relax around the pool, enjoy the spa or try their luck in the casino. Charles joined Katherine by the pool, but he spent the time reviewing reports and documents for his work.

Katherine had to admit her mind was on her job, as well. She had some ideas of things to say to Sadie, but needed to run them by her father, first. She wished she could talk to Charles, but he was engrossed in his reading and never liked to be interrupted.

She found herself watching for Tom. He was a good listener, the kind of person who could help her sort out her thoughts. But, with the ship under sail, he was probably on duty, and she saw no sign of him.

In the afternoon, Charles returned to the suite for a nap. But Katherine was too restless to sleep. She went for a walk and found herself drawn to the library. This, of course, was where Ariana had worked. Both the library and her quarters had been searched thoroughly after her disappearance, but had revealed no clues as to her whereabouts. She was to all appearances merely an ordinary young woman who had vanished from the face of the earth.

Katherine pushed open the door to the library and discovered the only other occupants were Giorgio Tzekas and Father Connelly, the priest hired as an antiquities lecturer. She drew back, hoping to slip away unseen. So far, this voyage she had managed to avoid running into Giorgio. But it was too late; the two men broke off their tense conversation and turned toward her.

"Good afternoon, Mrs. Stamos." Father Connelly nodded to her.

"Good afternoon," Giorgio echoed. "It's good to see you again, Katherine. When I saw you were booked for this voyage, I was hoping we'd run into each other."

Exactly what Katherine had been hoping *wouldn't* happen.

"Do you two know each other?" Father Connelly asked, clearly surprised.

"Not well," Katherine said, at the same time Giorgio said "Very well."

The priest looked more puzzled.

"Mr. Tzekas is the son of my father's best friend," Katherine explained, avoiding looking at the first officer, though she could feel his gaze on her.

"Katherine and I practically grew up together in Athens," Giorgio said, clearly enjoying her discomfort. "We even dated for a while. Instead of being Mrs. Charles Slater, she might have been Mrs. Giorgio Tzekas." He laughed, a harsh sound. "Then I wouldn't be working as a first officer on one of her father's ships, would I?"

"We only went out a few times," Katherine said coolly. She had been eighteen, home for the summer from school in London and looking forward to swimming, sailing and flirting with all the local boys. Her father had asked her to attend an awards dance with Giorgio as a favor to him.

She hadn't been very excited about the idea, remembering how much she'd disliked Giorgio the few times they'd seen each other as children. But, when he arrived to pick her up, dressed in a stylish suit and carrying a bouquet of flowers, her hopes for the evening had risen. Giorgio at twenty was much better looking than she remembered, and he had nice manners and was a good dancer.

Unfortunately, it was clear he had set his sights on the eldest daughter of Elias Stamos. The day after the dance, he called on her again. And again. He wouldn't accept no for an answer and seemed determined to occupy all her time that summer.

When she resisted, he only turned up the pressure. He sent flowers and showed up at her house at all times of the day and night. She couldn't go anywhere without finding him there. When she agreed to go out to dinner with him, intending to use the opportunity to tell him in no uncertain terms that she would not see him again, he took her acceptance as a sign of encouragement. After the meal, he drove her to a lonely park known as the local make-out spot and began kissing and fondling her. She had to literally fight him off.

Terrified and shaking, she'd called a friend to take her home. She had never told her father what had happened, too ashamed, and more than a little afraid of what he might do. But she had refused to have anything else to do with Giorgio. Thankfully, she had had no occasion to see him again, until now.

She retreated toward the door. "I'll come back another time," she said. "I didn't mean to interrupt you."

"No interruption at all," Giorgio said. "I was just leaving." He moved past her, deliberately brushing his body against hers.

Katherine stood there awkwardly, wanting to leave, as well, but afraid, if she did so now, she'd find Giorgio waiting for her in the hallway.

"Is there something I can help you with, Mrs. Stamos?" Father Connelly asked. His eyes were filled with concern.

She debated telling him the whole story of her previous relationship with Giorgio. He was, after all, a priest. Perhaps, he could offer advice as to how to handle being on the ship with him now. But years of reticence kept her silent. Besides, the library reminded her of other things she could discuss with Father Connelly. "Do you remember Ariana Bennett?" she asked.

"The librarian who left the ship in Naples?" He sorted through the papers in the folder he held. "I didn't know her well, but I certainly knew of her."

"I understand she had an interest in antiquities and wondered if she'd ever discussed this with you."

For a moment, Father Connelly looked alarmed, but the expression was soon veiled. "She attended some of my lectures and, once, asked me about the replicas on display here in the library." He indicated the items in a glass case at one end of the room. "She was more knowledgeable than most. I understand her father was a collector."

"He was a museum curator."

"That's right." The priest's expression grew grave. "I remember now. He came to a sad end. Arrested for smuggling antiquities and died in police custody. The poor young woman was quite grieved by this. I did my best to offer words of comfort, to reassure her that, despite what some believe, the sins of the fathers are not visited upon their children."

"She confided in you?" Katherine asked. The news surprised her. Ariana had struck her as the private sort, not one to discuss her family tragedy with others.

Father Connelly's smile struck Katherine as more of a smirk. "I am a priest. It's one of my duties to listen to people's confidences."

"Then did she mention what she intended to do in Naples? Did she give any indication that she was leaving the ship for good?"

He shook his head. "She did not. Perhaps she met someone when she went ashore and decided to stay with him for a while." He shrugged. "Young people can be very unpredictable." He made a slight bow. "If you'll excuse me, I must go and prepare for the lecture I'm to give tomorrow. It was a pleasure talking with you."

The new librarian, Margery, entered the library as Father Connelly was leaving. She greeted him, then turned to Katherine. "Is there anything I can help you with?" she asked. She was a pretty, dark-haired young woman with a quiet, efficient manner.

"Did you know the librarian who was here before you, Ariana Bennett?" Katherine asked.

Margery shook her head. "No. I heard she'd left the ship without telling anyone." She shrugged. "She probably had a boyfriend she wanted to stay with. It happens." She sat behind her desk at one end of the room. "Let me know if I can help you find anything."

Katherine sat in a chair across from the display case and studied the items there. She knew little about ancient artifacts so, to her, the vase, tablet, coin and other pieces in the case were merely beautiful objects. She couldn't have distinguished these replicas from the real items that fetched hundreds of thousands of dollars at auctions.

To Ariana, these objects might have held more meaning. Were they the sort of thing her father was accused of smuggling? She must have looked at these every time she came to work and thought of him. Did she— as Sadie had suggested—really set out to prove his innocence? In Naples?

But what in Naples would have a connection to Ariana's father?

Katherine shook her head and stood once more. The mystery of Ariana's disappearance was engrossing, and a natural concern for her both as a mother of a young woman and as the person most responsible for the public image of *Alexandra's Dream*. But she was wise enough to see that it also provided a distraction from her biggest concern—the state of her marriage.

She walked to the shelves and studied the offerings

there. It was probably too much to hope for that a cruise ship's library would have any self-help books aimed at repairing troubled relationships. People didn't like to think of such things in paradise.

She was still scanning the shelves for something of interest when the door swung open and June swept into the room. "Hello there," June called cheerily. "How are you today?"

"I'm fine," Katherine said. "How are you? You're looking well."

June was wearing a dark blue one-piece bathing suit under a knee-length gauzy black cover-up, sandals decorated with sea shells and a very large straw hat. "I just came to pick up another one of these wonderful romances," she said, heading for the bookcase of well-thumbed paperbacks that could be borrowed on the honor system. She chose a book from a low shelf. The paperback had a bright red cover and a picture of a man and woman embracing.

"You're a fan of romance novels?" Katherine asked.

"Oh, my, yes." June clutched the book to her chest and grinned. "They're so entertaining. And who doesn't like to be reminded of what it's like to fall in love?"

Maybe that's what I need, Katherine thought. *A reminder of what it's like.*

June leaned closer, her tone confidential. "Besides, these books have done wonders for my marriage."

Katherine stared at the little red paperback. "They have?"

"Absolutely. You know what one of the secrets to a happy marriage is, don't you?"

Katherine started to shake her head and thought better of it. "I'm sure there are a lot of things that go into a happy marriage," she said. "Respect, communication, common goals…"

"Yes, yes, yes, all that certainly." June fluttered her hand impatiently. "But one thing that fosters all that is great sex."

Katherine stared at the petite octogenarian before her, too dumbfounded to speak. Did a woman June's age really think much about such things?

"You're shocked, I can tell," June said. She laughed. "You young people think you invented sex? Or that people my age can't enjoy it? I'll let you in on a little secret, dear. I may move a little more slowly than I used to and it may take a while for things to heat up, but, once they do, sex can be just as wonderful—even more wonderful—than it was when I was your age."

"It…it can?" Katherine stammered.

"Of course. Haven't you heard that sixty percent of sex takes place in your mind? And my mind works just fine, thank you very much." She held up the book. "Of course, it never hurts to have a little inspiration."

"Inspiration?" Katherine felt like an idiot, repeating everything June said, but she couldn't seem to find any other words.

"Yes. Reading these stories puts me in the mood, and then I can put Albert in the mood." A devilish look crept into her eyes. "Sometimes I even read the love scenes to him. He quite likes that."

Katherine refrained from clapping her hands over her ears, though she was clearly learning more about her elderly friends than she wanted to know. "That's great," she said weakly.

"You should try it, dear," June advised, her expression serious. "I remember how it is at your age. Things can begin to seem a little stale if you don't do something to shake them up." She turned to the shelf and plucked a book from the row of paperbacks. "This one is very good. Lots of action and romance. And hot sex. Just the thing to add some spice to your life. You read it and see if I'm not right."

Katherine stared at the book. The gorgeous man and woman on the cover were obviously enjoying each other quite a lot. "I'll give it a try," she said.

"You do that." June waved and sailed out of the room.

Katherine looked at the book again, tempted to put it back on the shelf. Charles was something of a literature snob and would likely make fun of her if he saw her reading this.

But June had said it would help. And she definitely needed help. She wasn't ready to give up on her marriage yet, but she was running out of ideas. If she and Charles couldn't find a way to be close again, what was the point of staying together? If this little paperback was what she needed, then she was more than willing to give it a try.

CHAPTER SIX

ELIAS JOINED THE CRUISE in Naples, moving into the penthouse suite next to Katherine and Charles and arranging for a private meeting with Sadie Bennett and Katherine that evening.

"It's a pleasure to meet you at last, Mrs. Bennett," Elias said, taking Sadie's hand when she arrived at the door of his quarters. "I hope you have been comfortable on *Alexandra's Dream.*"

"Thank you. I'm as comfortable as I could be anywhere, with my daughter still missing."

Elias released her hand. "Of course. We are all distressed at Miss Bennett's disappearance." He ushered Sadie into the living room, where Katherine waited.

Katherine thought Sadie looked exhausted, her skin pale, dark circles shadowing her eyes. "Hello, Sadie," she said, her voice gentle. "Thank you for agreeing to meet with us."

"If nothing else, I wanted to meet you and thank you again for your kindness," Sadie said to Elias. "I was touched by your concern."

"Indeed, we are concerned," Elias said. "I am doing everything in my power to locate your daughter."

"Have you done everything?" Sadie hugged her arms across her stomach. "You haven't contacted the press. Surely, the media can help us." Her voice rose, agitated. "They can broadcast Ariana's picture and information about her to a wide audience. Someone must have seen her that last day in Naples. Maybe they saw someone with her."

"Please, sit down." Elias indicated the sofa.

After a moment's hesitation, Sadie sat, perched on the edge of the cushion, as if, at any moment, she might flee.

Elias sat in a chair angled toward her. "The police in Naples conducted extensive interviews and learned nothing," he said.

"So they say." Sadie looked away. "I visited them this morning."

"What did they tell you?" Katherine asked. She stood behind her father, gripping the back of his upholstered chair.

"They were very solicitous," Sadie said. "But mostly, they seemed to want to reassure me that none of this was their fault. They have adopted the attitude that Ariana ran off with a young man. Or away from a love affair that ended badly." She looked at Elias again, her expression fierce. "I know my daughter. She would not have done anything like that."

Elias nodded. "No, she did not strike me as an irresponsible young woman."

Sadie's shoulders sagged. "I'm grateful you believe me. And I understand you fear this story could bring a bad reputation to your cruise line, but I must put my daughter first."

"Of course I don't want bad press for *Alexandra's Dream*," he said. "A story like this could easily ruin our reputation. But, if I truly thought the media could help us, I would not hesitate to involve them."

Sadie frowned. "Why don't you believe going to the press would help?"

Elias leaned forward, elbows on his knees. "I'm afraid it would put your daughter in danger," he said.

Sadie's eyes widened. "Danger?"

"If she has met with bad people, they might see publicity as an attack against them," Elias said. "They could take their anger out on Ariana."

Sadie's face turned the color of milk and Katherine feared she would faint. Elias took Sadie's hand in his. "I apologize," he said. "I don't mean to frighten you. I'm only trying to be honest. We don't know what has happened to Ariana, so we must be very careful not to act rashly."

Katherine moved around to sit on the other side of her friend. "Sadie, if anyone sympathizes with what you're going through, it's me," she said. "My daughter, Gemma, is not that much younger than Ariana. In your shoes, I'd be frantic, as well. But also think about what the kind of publicity you're talking about could do to Ariana's reputation even if she isn't in danger."

Sadie turned to look at Katherine. "I don't understand."

"All these rumors circulating about her having run off with some man, or having been involved in an affair that came to a bad end would be printed in the papers along with news of her disappearance," Katherine ex-

plained. "There would be speculation as to her charac-
ter and news of her father's arrest. The charges against
him would no doubt be dredged up. The press might
even try to paint her as guilty of the same crimes."

Sadie's head drooped. "I hadn't thought..." She
nodded. "You're right. After Derek was arrested, the
stories in the news were horrible. I couldn't pick up the
paper or turn on the TV without seeing another story
about him. Some of them made the wildest accusations."

"Unfortunately, a young woman would be even more
vulnerable to such accusations," Elias said.

She nodded again, then took a deep breath and
straightened. "Then, what are we to do?"

"I've hired a new investigator," Elias said. "We will
renew our efforts to locate your daughter. No avenue
will be left unexplored. And I will keep you informed
of everything."

When Sadie's gaze fixed on Elias, Katherine recognized the moment she began to trust him. Some of the
stiffness went out of her shoulders and something like
hope flickered in her eyes.

As for Elias, Katherine sensed in him a true affection for the American widow. As he continued to hold
Sadie's hand and offer words of comfort, Katherine
studied him more closely. He was a handsome man, his
curly dark hair shot through with silver and his eyes a
rich brown. He had the tan, weathered face of a man
who spent time out of doors and had kept himself slim
and fit.

Sadie, likewise, was a very attractive woman. Could

it be that her father's concern was based on more than sympathy for a fellow human being and a desire to protect his business? Was he attracted to Ariana's mother?

Katherine rejected the idea. Elias had loved Alexandra so completely. Ten years had passed without him even dating. Whatever she'd seen in his expression as he held Sadie's hand had been a passing fancy of her own imagination—no doubt, brought on by reading the romance novel June had pressed on her. Though she had to admit, she was enjoying the book quite a bit.

Sadie stood at last and Elias escorted her to the door. "We will talk again," he said. "Try not to worry. Rest."

"I'll try. And thank you again for all your help."

"That went well, I thought," Katherine said when he joined her again.

"Yes." He gave her a look of approval. "I never would have thought of all that about Ariana's reputation. And what's this about her father?"

"Ariana's father, Derek Bennett, was arrested and charged with smuggling antiquities," Katherine explained. "I suppose his position as a museum curator made it easy for him to get such items. He died in police custody, before he could come to trial. Ariana and he were apparently very close. Sadie thinks her daughter came on the cruise not only to visit places her father had loved, but perhaps in hopes of clearing his name."

Elias frowned. "Where could the girl be? It's as if she vanished. The last anyone saw of her, she was asking directions to the diggings at Paestum."

"Do you think something bad has happened to her?" The lines around his mouth and along his forehead became more pronounced. "I wouldn't say anything to upset Sadie, but my contacts tell me some of those diggings are controlled by the mob, the Camorra. If Ariana stumbled into one of their operations…" He shook his head. "We may never find her again."

Katherine put her hand to her heart, as if to still the wild rhythm his words engendered. She could too easily put herself in Sadie's shoes, terrified that some harm had come to Gemma. "What can we do?"

"We'll keep looking," Elias said. "Mrs. Bennett deserves to know what happened to her daughter."

She nodded. It was terrible, feeling this helpless. How much more terrible for Sadie.

"Now, tell me," Elias said, his expression less somber. "How have things been with you? Have you been enjoying your vacation?"

"Until this, yes. I explored Kusadasi the other day. Such a beautiful place."

"I'm sure Charles enjoyed the ruins at Ephesus. There's some fascinating architecture there."

She shifted in her seat, avoiding her father's gaze. "Charles didn't accompany me. He stayed behind to work."

"Damn it, the whole idea of this trip was for you both to get away from work. To spend time with each other."

Though she kept her composure, inwardly, Katherine cringed at her father's vehemence. "I know," she said. "But it doesn't seem to be happening." She was beginning to think she and Charles had forgotten *how* to be alone together.

"Then, make it happen. If I have to, I'll strand you

two on a deserted island. Then you'll have no choice but to spend time together. Don't think I won't do it, either."

· "Why is this so important to you?" she asked, raising her eyes to meet his. "Is it because you don't believe in divorce?"

"Has it come to that, then? Would you really divorce him?"

She looked away. "I don't know," she answered truthfully. "But what is the point of staying married if we can't even communicate anymore?"

"Do you believe there's another woman?"

The question caught her off guard. "No." She'd considered the idea, but even though Charles traveled extensively, she'd seen no sign of anyone else in his life.

"And he doesn't drink excessively or gamble or lie or beat you?"

"No!" Charles was the most temperate, truly kind man she knew.

Elias's expression softened. "If I thought divorce was the best thing for you, I wouldn't hesitate to stand behind you. But Charles is a good man. I believe he loves you, and I believe you still love him." He took her hand. "You know I loved your mother very much."

"I know. But maybe everyone doesn't have that kind of love."

"Everyone deserves a chance at it. When I think of the years you and Charles have spent together, of Gemma and the home you've made… I want to see you give that a chance. A real chance." He released her hand. "Don't let your marriage die because of indifference. Fight for it."

"I will." She nodded. "I'll plan a special evening with him while we're on the cruise." An evening when they would really talk. And really listen to each other for a change. Maybe that was all they needed to recapture the love they'd once known.

TASIA CATOMERIS considered it her business to keep up with her son's father. Elias Stamos had shut her out of his life before Theo was even born, but the very fact of Theo's birth tied them to each other for life, whether Elias accepted this or not.

At least he had finally acknowledged Theo, his only son, though all his attentions now could never make up for his years of neglect. "Have you heard from your father lately?" Tasia asked Theo whenever he passed through Athens, as he had this day, on one of his frequent trips from his new home in Florida to oversee his tour company in Corfu.

"I talked to him a few days ago," Theo said. "We discussed meeting in St. Tropez for lunch."

"What are you going to be doing in St. Tropez?" she asked.

"A businessman there is interested in supporting my efforts to save the wild horses of Kefalonia. It's someone Trish knows through her work. I'm going to meet with him."

Tasia suspected Theo wanted her to ask about the well-being of his girlfriend, but she really had little interest in the woman. Another pampered American who clearly wasn't good enough for her son. But he was besotted enough to follow her halfway across the world to the United States to live with her most of each year. Tasia hated the idea, but Theo had ignored all her protestations.

"And Elias?" she asked. "What business has he in St. Tropez?" Though she and Elias both lived in Athens, they seldom saw each other. She had long suspected guilt kept him away. That and a desire to keep the existence of a former lover and their son a secret from his oh-so-respectable wife and daughters. What a blow it must have been to those young women to learn they weren't their father's only children, though sadly, their mother had been dead and gone years before Elias's shameful secret was made public.

"He's joining one of his cruises for a while," Theo said. He helped himself to a drink from the bar she kept well stocked for herself and her business associates. Though Theo was taller than his father, he had the same thick curly hair and muscular build. And certain mannerisms—the way he held the drink decanter as he poured, a certain swagger in his walk—recalled her former lover so strongly that Tasia had to bite her tongue to keep from calling him Elias.

The idea grated. After all, she'd raised the boy by herself, with the help of her family, of course. Elias had contributed nothing but his sperm—and a few token dollars to assuage his conscience.

"Did he decide he needed a vacation?" she asked with a smirk. The man's whole life had been a vacation.

Theo shook his head. "It has something to do with that woman who disappeared a few weeks ago."

"What woman was that?"

"You remember—the ship's librarian from *Alexandra's Dream?* I thought I told you."

"Maybe you did. There wasn't anything in the news about it."

"No. Elias made sure the press didn't get hold of the story."

"I'm sure he did. The man is ruthless when it comes to business." Ruthless in his personal relationships, as well. Money and privilege made such coldness easier.

Theo looked at her oddly. He never liked when she criticized his father, though he, of all people, had every reason to hate Elias, who had, after all, had nothing to do with Theo for most of his life. It was only when his precious cruise ship business had stood to lose money because of Theo's tour company withdrawing a contract that Elias had seen fit to publicly acknowledge his son.

"What has happened now?" she asked. "Have they found the woman?"

"I don't think so. Apparently, her mother is on the ship, making trouble. Elias wants to meet with her, attempt to calm her down."

"No doubt, he will." He had a smooth way about him. Men with money and breeding and those cultured manners Elias had could impress many women, especially dowdy American housewives such as this Mrs. Bennett must be. "I'm sure he'll charm the worried American and have her swooning over him like all the other women in his life, then he'll sail away, on to the next conquest."

Theo stared at her. "I don't think Elias has been involved with any woman since Alexandra died. At least that's what his daughters told me."

"That's what he wants people to believe, I'm sure. He likes playing the role of devoted husband, grieving for the love of his life. But I know better." Elias used his looks and charm and money to get any woman he wanted. He wasn't the type of man to ever commit to one woman, though he was committed enough to Alexandra's money.

If Tasia had had money, it would have been a different story, she was sure. She had not met a man yet she could not control. Except for Elias.

"When you see him, tell him I said hello," she told Theo. She liked to remind Elias that she was still here. The one woman who had given him what every man wanted most—a son. The one woman he had never truly been able to control.

WHEN ALEXANDRA'S DREAM docked in Livorno, Sadie joined a group of passengers on a tour of Florence. The piazzas, churches and gardens of this gem of Tuscany drew exclamations and much snapping of pictures from her fellow passengers, but Sadie could only think of how much Ariana would have enjoyed taking this tour with her. Together, mother and daughter would have had a memorable day. Instead, Sadie had a hard time shaking the sadness that threatened to overwhelm her even in these beautiful surroundings.

While the other women in her group descended on the local outlet mall to shop for leather jackets, shoes and fine jewelry, Sadie opted to return to the ship early. As she boarded, she was surprised to see Father Connelly ahead of her. The priest struggled with a large box and she rushed to assist him. "Let me help you, Father," she said, holding open a door for him.

"Thank you." He gave her a distracted smile and hurried past her, his purchase cradled in his arms.

Curious to see what could be so important that he wouldn't stop to chat—and grateful for any distraction—Sadie followed him. He went into the library and she entered after him.

She found him at the desk, the box open and something wrapped in many layers of paper in front of him. He looked up, startled. "Mrs. Bennett, is there something you need?"

"I was curious to see what you purchased in Livorno." She nodded toward the paper-wrapped bundle.

He hesitated, then his expression relaxed. "I couldn't resist adding to my collection of reproductions." He nodded toward the lighted case at the end of the library. "Florence had some very fine replicas of ancient pieces. It was difficult to choose only one."

"May I see?" She moved closer.

He hesitated, then said, "Certainly." He carefully unwound the paper until a small statue of a male figure was revealed. "It's a terra-cotta antefix, or roof ornament," he explained. He ran a hand lovingly over the figure. "It depicts Neptune, or Poseidon as he was known to the Greeks. The God of the sea."

Sadie studied the small figure of a bearded man. He carried a trident in one hand and his arm was upraised, though the hand had broken off. Traces of black and red paint adorned the pinkish clay of the terra-cotta. "It looks very old," she said.

"Yes. The artist did a very nice job of reproducing the original artifact." He began wrapping the figure in paper once more. "I will have to find the perfect place in the case to display this."

Sadie turned to look at the rest of his collection. "You certainly have some fine pieces," she said. "I would think some of these could fool experts."

He frowned. "I assure you, Mrs. Bennett," he said stiffly. "No one is trying to fool anyone here."

"I would never suggest that you were." She, of all people, was sensitive to accusations of wrongdoing in this area. "I only meant that I appreciate your efforts to acquire very faithful representations."

"Yes. Since I can't afford the real thing, I content myself with acquiring faithful reproductions." He joined her in front of the case. "I enjoy looking at them, plus they are useful in my educational lectures. You must attend one of my lectures while you're here," he said. "People tell me they're very entertaining."

"I'm sure they are." She didn't want to insult him by telling him she had had little interest in ancient artifacts while Derek was alive, and even less since his arrest and death. Instead, she said, "It's wonderful that *Alexandra's Dream* offers a program like this. I'm sure it's unique among cruises in the area."

"Elias Stamos is very interested in promoting local culture," Father Connelly said. "He understands the importance of educating people as well as encouraging the preservation of fine objects such as these." He smiled. "I'm happy to do what I can to assist him in those efforts."

Elias Stamos again. The man had been much in her

thoughts today. Though she had looked forward to their meeting as another way for her to help her daughter, she had not been prepared for how handsome he was, or the way the soft timbre of his voice sent tremors through her. When he'd taken her hand in his, she'd felt warmed through by his touch, and his eyes when he'd looked into hers had been filled with such kindness she'd had to fight back tears.

This onslaught of emotion had almost overwhelmed her, and it had taken all her efforts to shift her focus once more to pleading her case to take Ariana's story to the media.

But Elias's assertion that doing so might place her daughter in danger, and Katherine's reminder that alerting the media invited them to publish every sordid rumor from Ariana and Derek's past, had deterred her. Her only hope now lay with the new investigator Elias had hired.

"Is there anything else I can help you with?" Father Connelly asked, interrupting her thoughts.

"No." She shook her head. "No, thank you." Only Ariana's return would truly help her. In the meantime, she had placed her trust in Elias, a man, who, in many ways, seemed larger than life, like the very Greek gods portrayed in these artifacts. If only he really did have the power to direct human actions and ensure a happy ending for them all.

THOUGH KATHERINE had promised her father she would renew her efforts to spend time alone with Charles, to work on recapturing the closeness they had once enjoyed, that was proving more difficult than she'd anticipated.

For one thing, too many people turned to her for advice and comfort: June Westcott sought her opinion on the appropriate dress to wear to dinner and which shore excursions would be most enjoyable, while Sadie Bennett relied on Katherine for sympathy and comfort when she fretted about her missing daughter. Even the crew sought her out. The caterer wanted her approval for a new menu design and the entertainment staff requested she mediate in a disagreement about scheduling.

Then there was the fact that, though Charles had made a genuine effort to put aside work for the duration of the trip, he received almost daily e-mails asking for his urgent answer to any number of questions. He had vowed not to check his e-mail in order to be left in peace, but then Gemma had written to ask his opinion on which topic she should choose for a paper for one of her classes. Since he could deny his daughter nothing, he checked his e-mail regularly in order to be available to her when she needed him.

Which meant that even now he was trying to solve a problem with a supplier in Berlin while Katherine attempted to finish the romance novel June had urged on her.

But, though the book had held her interest yesterday, today the words blurred on the page. She had received her own e-mail from Gemma this morning. Two cryptic lines:

Hi, Mom. Too busy to write much. Classes are going well and I met this really hot guy!

Not the words a mother wanted to read when she was hundreds of miles away at sea. Not that Gemma hadn't dated before. She was a beautiful, popular girl. But she was too young to be getting involved in a relationship, especially when she ought to be concentrating on her studies.

But what bothered Katherine more than the unsettling news about the "hot guy" was the lack of details. Gemma had always confided in her about everything—school gossip, summer crushes and the minutiae of everyday life. While other mothers lamented their teenager's reluctance to communicate with them, Katherine had been elated that Gemma had been willing, even eager, to share so much of herself with her mother.

The idea that Gemma didn't have time to share these details now hurt. Objectively, she realized this was part of her daughter growing up, of severing the apron strings, but, emotionally, she grieved the loss.

She resolutely pushed thoughts of her daughter aside and focused on the book once more.

"Thank you, dear. How did I get so lucky to marry such a thoughtful man."

"I'm the one who's lucky, with a wife like you. Turn over and I'll rub lotion on your back. You wouldn't want to burn."

"You're so thoughtful. Isn't this the most beautiful day? Can you imagine anywhere more wonderful?"

"Where I am doesn't matter, as long as I'm with you."

The dialogue was not from the pages of the book Katherine was reading, but from the couple who had taken up two chaise lounges nearby on the sundeck. Saccharine as it might be, she had no doubt of the feeling behind the words of the two newlyweds who gazed at each other with the starry-eyed looks of those who believe they have discovered and perfected true love.

She shifted lower in her chair and read another paragraph. But the couple there were also madly in love— though their dialogue was more original. They shared their deepest emotions and dreams with each other, then confirmed their feelings with enthusiastic lovemaking that left Katherine exhausted and feeling defeated.

She had heard the criticism that such books were unrealistic, but that was not why she laid aside the novel. She could remember a time when she and Charles had been just as close, their lovemaking just as earnest and energetic. How or why they had lost all that disturbed her. Over the years they had spent less time together, each focused on other things. The closeness had slipped away and now it was as if everything was conspiring to continue to keep them apart.

The newlyweds began kissing, sharing one lounger now in a public display Katherine had no desire to watch. She donned her cover-up, gathered her belongings and left the sundeck. Charles was in the room working, so she didn't want to go there.

She ended up in the tearoom, where she ordered a pot of Earl Grey and contemplated her mother's portrait.

She had never thought much about her parents' marriage while her mother had been alive. That they were together and always would be was a fact of life, as immutable as the sun rising every morning. As personalities, they were not a great deal alike, her father assertive, even abrasive at times, an outdoorsman, driven and competitive.

Alexandra had been the refined, gentle English rose who, nevertheless, revealed her thorns when crossed. She was not afraid to stand up to her husband and, to anyone who knew them well, it was clear that she held the true power in the household.

When Alexandra had been diagnosed with the cancer that would end her life, she'd spent her few remaining months doing everything in her power to relieve her family's suffering. She entreated them not to mourn and reminded them she would always be with them, in their memories and in the sounds of the wind and the sea that she loved.

Katherine swallowed a knot of tears, remembering her mother's words. If only Alexandra were with her now, she was sure she'd have the right advice to give her—about Gemma and about Charles.

Immediately after Alexandra had died, Elias had continued his usual routines. He'd worked in the office, he'd visited his daughters. Everyone had spoke of how well he'd been doing, and Katherine'd secretly wondered if he'd really loved her mother very much at all.

Then, more than a year after Alexandra's passing, grief had hit Elias with a tidal wave that was felt throughout the family. The man who had devoted himself to business went days without going into the office. Travel and sailing, two things he had loved his whole life, no longer interested him. Months stretched into years, and Katherine and her sister, Helena, had begun to fear he might never recover. It had taken their combined efforts to pull him from his grief and interest him in business again.

With the launching of *Alexandra's Dream,* Katherine began to feel her father had truly returned to his old self. If there was any difference now, it was that he had a softer nature. He was a little less brusque, a little more aware of the importance of family.

Which, no doubt, explained his interest in the health of her marriage to Charles.

She sipped her now-cold tea and studied her mother's portrait again. Alexandra was smiling in it, a subtle lift at the corners of her mouth, as if she knew a great secret.

What was your secret to a happy marriage, Mother? Katherine silently asked. But the portrait remained stubbornly unresponsive and the wind whispered no answer in her ear.

All those months of watching her father grieve had showed Katherine the depth of his love for Alexandra. A love she longed to feel in her own life—if only she knew how to create it or find it again.

The door to the tearoom opened and Giorgio entered. "I thought I saw you come in here," he said, striding toward Katherine's table.

She set down her cup and looked around for a way to make a graceful exit. But the only other people in the tearoom at this hour were strangers, and Giorgio was between her and the door. Resigned, she sat up straighter, took a deep breath and faced the last man she wanted to see.

CHAPTER SEVEN

GIORGIO WAS SMILING, sure of himself, his walk practically a swagger "What do you want?" Katherine asked.

Uninvited, he pulled out a chair and sat across from her. "Seeing you the other day reminded me how much I enjoyed the time we spent together when we were dating."

"We were never really dating," she said. "I only went out with you a few times."

"That's not how I remember it. We spent most of the summer together"

She had the impression he was telling the truth. In Giorgio's twisted mind, they had been practically lovers. She shuddered at the thought. "That was almost twenty years ago," she said, keeping her voice mild.

"Yes, and the years have been good to you, Katherine. You're looking lovely."

He reached across the table and tried to take her hand, but she pulled it away. "What are you doing?" she asked. "I'm a married woman."

He looked around the room. "Your husband isn't here now, is he?" His eyes met hers again, his smile more of a leer. "Since we're alone, I thought we might take the opportunity to get to know each other again. You know, our families always planned for us to be together. Too bad it didn't work out."

"I know no such thing." She stood, determined to end this conversation—and any fantasies he might be having about "getting to know her" again. "Any relationship you remember between the two of us is entirely in your imagination. I wasn't interested in you then and I'm not interested in you now. And, if you persist in following me around, I'll tell my father *everything* that happened that summer and you won't have this job anymore."

His expression darkened. "What does your father care about what happened twenty years ago? Besides, I'll tell him you're lying."

"Whom do you think he'll believe—you or his daughter?"

Not waiting for his answer, she started to move away from the table. He shot out a hand and captured her wrist, then faced her. "Don't say a word to Elias or you'll be sorry," he said.

"Let go of me. You're hurting me." She struggled to pull free.

"It's very important that I stay on this ship," he said, his voice low. "Don't say anything to your father or I'll tell your husband I saw you with Tom Diamantopoulos in Kusadasi."

She stiffened. "Charles knows Tom and I toured the city together."

"Maybe so. But I'll tell him you were doing more than touring." He smiled. "I'll tell him I saw you go into a hotel with Tom. That I saw you embracing in the lobby."

"That's a lie!"

"Yes, but I'm a good liar. I can make him believe me."

She wrenched away from him and ran to the door. She slowed in the hallway, even managing a weak smile and a nod to a passing couple. But, inside, she was shaking with rage and fear. Giorgio was crazy. But Charles might believe him. He was already suspicious of Tom, and he had to sense the growing distance in their marriage.

She glanced over her shoulder at the door to the tearoom. Giorgio had emerged, but had been stopped by the couple, who had engaged him in conversation. He looked up and his eyes caught hers, his expression no longer friendly, but threatening.

She hurried to the elevator and ducked inside, her mind racing. She pressed the button for twelve, the Helios sun deck. The beauty salon and spa were on this deck. Two places she was sure to be surrounded by other people—places where Giorgio wouldn't dare to follow.

"Welcome to the Jasmine Spa." An Asian woman with stylishly cut black hair greeted Katherine as she entered the salon. "How may I help you?"

"Katherine!" June rose from a chair on the other side of the low wall separating the reception area from the beauty salon and waved. "How nice to see you again."

Katherine smiled. "Hello, June. What are you here for?"

"I'm having my nails done. They do such a nice job."

"Is it possible I could have a manicure, also?" Katherine asked the receptionist. In her experience, appointments were booked quickly once the ship set sail, but occasionally there were cancellations.

The young woman consulted the appointment book. "We could fit you in now if you are ready," she said.

"That would be wonderful." Anything to buy time to make sure Giorgio had given up on pursuing her—at least for now.

"Would you like a pedicure, also?" the young woman asked.

Katherine nodded. "Why not?" It would be good to sit for a while and be pampered. And give her racing heart time to return to normal.

She followed the young woman to the pedicure chair next to June. A second Asian woman in a pink smock greeted her and explained the operation of the massage feature on the chair, then began to fill the foot basin with warm water.

"Isn't this wonderful?" June asked when Katherine was settled. "Such a treat."

"Yes, it is." She tried to pull her mind away from her unnerving encounter with Giorgio and focus on her friend. "How are you doing? Are you having a good cruise?"

"We're having a wonderful time, dear. Thank you." June's face was radiant. "Our children promised the trip of a lifetime and I think they're right. I don't know when Albert and I have enjoyed ourselves—and each other—more."

"That's saying a great deal, considering you've been together sixty years," Katherine said.

June laid her head back on the chair's neck rest and closed her eyes. "Sometimes it's difficult to remember a time without him—and sometimes it doesn't seem that long at all." The idea of spending a lifetime together was the ideal every newlywed couple started out with, Katherine supposed. But the reality of achieving that goal was much more difficult than she'd thought when she'd stood before the altar in a white satin gown and said "I do."

"Is Albert the only man you've ever loved?" she asked.

June opened her eyes again. "I was in love once before," she said. "Or what I thought of as love. I was sixteen and he was nineteen. We planned to spend our lives together, then he was killed in the war."

"Oh." The words were shocking, out of place in the luxurious surroundings. She tried to picture June as a heartbroken girl but failed. "I'm sorry. That must have been terrible for you."

June nodded. "It was. It was also very tragic and romantic and all of that." She turned her head to look at Katherine. "But young hearts heal quickly. By the time I met Albert four years later, I was beginning to realize that I hadn't known a great deal about love with my young soldier." She smiled. "I think people have the wrong idea about love altogether. At least they do about romantic love."

"What do you mean?" Katherine asked.

"We talk about love as something you 'fall into.' Like

a well or a trap. And then you stay there, in the same place for the rest of your life. But I think real love is more of a process of discovery. You're attracted to someone, they make you feel a certain way. And that attraction builds over time to an even deeper caring. But real love— the kind that takes you through the difficult times, through grieving and hardship and illness and all the other bad things life can throw your way—that kind of love takes time. It requires a maturity we can't have when we're young and there's still so much of life ahead of us."

At thirty-eight, Katherine had thought of herself as mature, but maybe not when it came to love. "I see what you mean," she said thoughtfully. "It can take a lifetime to really know another person."

"And sometimes we never really know them," June said. "But there's something to be said for keeping a little mystery in a relationship, I think. Then there's always the anticipation of learning something new." She sat up and admired her polished toenails. "Oh, that's really lovely, isn't it?"

"Very nice," Katherine said. She surrendered her own foot to the ministrations of the pedicurist. What new things did she have to learn about Charles?

And what things was she afraid to learn? Did he still love her? Did he want to spend the rest of his life with her? Did he think their marriage was worth working to save? Did *she* really want to save it?

There was a time when she was sure of the answers to those questions, but not anymore. She closed her eyes and leaned back against the headrest, willing the gentle vibration to ease the tension in her neck and shoulders.

But the tension in her heart would take more than a massage to ease. She needed to find the courage to learn the answers to the tough questions about her marriage and about herself.

SADIE WOKE EARLY the fifth morning of the cruise thinking not only of Ariana, but of Elias Stamos. He had been so reassuring when he spoke of throwing his considerable fortune and power behind the search for Ariana, but had he really meant this? Why should a man like Elias concern himself with a young woman who everyone else thought had vanished in the wake of a disastrous love affair, or to follow a new lover? Perhaps he'd said what he had merely to placate a troublesome woman.

But, when she closed her eyes, she could still feel the warmth of his hand grasping hers, the balm of his concern washing over her. Surely, his concern had been genuine and he was going to help her.

Sleep having deserted her, she rose and dressed. She was drinking coffee and trying to decide what to do that day when a knock at her door startled her. Opening it, she found a steward bearing a note on a silver tray. Puzzled, she slit open the fine linen envelope and found a brief message.

Would you do me the honor of accompanying me today on a tour of Rome? It would give us the opportunity to talk more and to get to know each other better. Elias Stamos.

She stared at the words, her stomach fluttering with nerves and excitement. She could think of few things she'd like better than to spend the day in the company of a handsome, educated man, but she was so out of prac-tice at being with a man that she was as nervous as a girl.

"One moment, while I write my answer," she told the steward. She hurried to the desk in her room and found writing paper with the ship's monogram and penned a quick note accepting Elias's invitation and suggest-ing they meet at ten o'clock in the main lounge. She smiled as she handed it to the steward, thinking how old-fashioned it was to communicate like this in an age of e-mail and instant messages. Old-fashioned and somehow romantic, as well.

ARIANA SLUMPED against the wall of the sea cave, mo-mentarily stunned by the repercussions of the blast. The yacht she and Dante had been on only moments before had burst into flames, the roar of the fire audible even over the waves pounding the rocks. Had Dante saved their lives by insisting they get off the boat?

She looked around for her captor and saw him sprawled on the sandbar in front of the caves. She gave a cry and struggled to her feet and rushed to him. Putting a hand to his head, she felt something wet and sticky. Blood. A rock or some piece of debris must have struck him.

He turned toward her and groaned, and relief rushed through her. He was alive. Soon, he'd be awake.

And she would be gone. Though, in many ways, he had been nothing but kind to her during their enforced stay together, he had refused to let her leave or to contact her mother. She stood and looked down on his face, handsome even in repose, and felt a tug at her heart. She would never forget the way he had carried her so tenderly through the water, not ridiculing her fear or forcing her to do what she could not bring herself to do. She had felt so safe and cared for in his arms.

But that moment of tenderness did not make up for the fact that he had kidnapped her and refused to let her go, she reminded herself. The way he had repeatedly questioned her about her father and her knowledge of antiquities and smuggling made her more certain than ever that he was a member of a smuggling ring, himself, and maybe even part of the Camorra, though his actions on the yacht just now made that more difficult to believe.

She had to get away, and before he awoke. If she could make her way around to the fishing village on the other side of the island, she could contact her mother and her friends on *Alexandra's Dream*. And she could continue to search for evidence to clear her father's name.

She verified that her iPod in its waterproof case was still all right, then took a steadying breath and began making her way across the rocks, staying as close to shore as she could and hurrying as much as possible. Every few yards she looked back. Dante was more awake now, struggling to rise and shaking his head as if he was still dazed.

As she watched, he pulled himself to his feet and looked around. She saw his mouth open, though the sound of his voice was swallowed up by the crashing waves. She imagined he was calling for her. He would look first in the cave where he had left her, then he would no doubt start making his own way down the coastline, back toward the village. She had to find another place to hide, and soon.

She looked up, searching for some way to climb up, away from the water, but the cliffs here were almost perpendicular. She'd have to keep skirting them until she came to more gently sloping land.

Conscious of Dante still within sight, she tried to move faster, thwarted by the rocks and waves, which made it impossible to move more than a few feet without slipping and falling. She was soon soaking wet, her legs and arms slashed by sharp rock and coral, her eyes stinging from salt.

A sharp report rang out as she fell once more, and she cursed the wave that sloshed over her, momentarily blinding her and flooding her with panic. As she struggled to rise, another report sounded and a shard flew from a rock just in front of her.

She screamed as she realized someone was aiming at her and flung herself flat in the shallows, not caring now that water washed over her, praying only that the surrounding rocks would provide sufficient cover against whoever was shooting at her.

"Ariana!" Dante's voice carried over the waves, and she risked raising her eyes a few inches. She saw him heading toward her. Evidently, the shooter had drawn attention to her location.

She looked around wildly for somewhere—

anywhere—to flee. But the shooter had her pinned down.

Now Dante was shooting back at their unseen assailant. Could Ariana risk making a run for it while the shooter was distracted? Or was she well and truly caught between an enemy she did not know and the enemy she did?

CHAPTER EIGHT

ELIAS WAS WAITING for Sadie when she arrived in the main lounge later that morning. Dressed in tan linen trousers and a white button-down shirt with the sleeves rolled to the elbows, he made a striking figure in the ornate lounge. Posed as he was among statues of Aphrodite, Artemis, Athena and Poseidon, he might have been one more Greek god come to life in modern dress.

She scolded herself for such fancy and hurried to meet him.

"Mrs. Bennett, I'm so glad you could join me." The genuine delight in his smile flattered her. "Rome is one of my favorite cities, but it's much more enjoyable if I can share it with someone."

"If we're going to be spending the day together, you must call me Sadie," she said.

"And you must call me Elias."

"Of course." The words earned her an even more dazzling smile that made her stomach flutter.

"I've never been to Rome," she said as they exited the lounge. "I've never been much of anywhere, really."

"As you can imagine, I've traveled a great deal, though much of it has been related to my business." He glanced at her, his eyes smiling. "You've given me an excuse to enjoy a brief holiday."

She knew very well he had not suddenly joined the cruise for a holiday, but she let the comment pass. "Thank you for inviting me to accompany you," she said. "I'd like to see the city and, truthfully, I'm grateful for the distraction."

A private car was waiting for them at the dock in Civitavecchia to take them to Rome. The ride through the Etruscan countryside passed quickly, as Elias asked her about her home in Philadelphia. They discovered a shared love of classical music and spent the rest of the journey discussing favorite composers and compositions.

Once in Rome, Sadie was struck by the great age of everything they passed. "It makes me feel rather insignificant, when I think how long some of these buildings have been here," she said as they passed a church that looked as if it might have sat on that spot since the beginning of Christianity.

"The buildings mean little without the history of the people associated with them," Elias said. "Though my son-in-law, being an architect, would no doubt argue their architectural merit."

"Will you think me terrible if I tell you the layers of dirt coating them detracts from their charm for me?"

He laughed, a hearty, masculine sound that sent a tremor of desire through her. "My late wife was the same way," he said.

"Was she American, also? I understand we have a reputation for being too particular about cleanliness."

"No, she was English, but she despised dirt." He gestured toward a street ahead. "As long as you're here, you must see the Trevi Fountain."

They made their way down cobbled streets and across a square filled with tourists and pigeons to the famous fountain. Elias offered to take her picture in front of the landmark, then prevailed upon a passerby to take his photo with her. As they stood before the fountain, his arm draped lightly across her shoulder, she felt a surge of longing for this to be more than a moment frozen in time. She wanted to feel his arm around her again and again, the way a woman feels the arm of a man with whom she has a long and close acquaintance.

The idea surprised her. She had not thought of a man that way in many years. While Ariana was still little, Sadie had suspected her husband was unfaithful. Derek spent many weeks away from home, tending to his duties as a museum curator, traveling the world to acquire new treasures for the museum's collection. But, even when he was home, there was a distance about him. A separateness that was present even in their bedroom. When she questioned him, he apologized and said he was distracted by work, but as months and years passed with little change, Sadie became more convinced that the love they had once known was lost forever.

The knowledge had hurt her. She had contemplated divorce, but some part of her heart remained tied to him, hoping things might one day be different. And she wanted to spare Ariana the pain of spending even less time with the father she adored.

So she had devoted herself to motherhood and to

going to concerts and volunteering with various charities. She had thought the part of her that could be attracted to a man had been killed by her husband's
indifference. Yet, Elias had awakened it again, suddenly
and surprisingly and at such an inopportune time.

How could she think of her own needs when her
daughter was missing? And was there really a spark between her and this man she'd just met, or did she feel
this way only because she was lonely and afraid and he
was someone strong she could lean on? Someone who
had promised to use all his considerable resources to
help her find her daughter.

They strolled around the fountain, studying the carvings of Neptune riding his shell chariot pulled by raging
sea horses. "The statues in the niches depict *Abundance*
and *Salubrity*," Elias explained.

Sadie stared at *Salubrity*, who offered a cup to a
snake, and shivered.

"Do you have a coin?" Elias asked. "You must throw
a coin in the fountain."

Before she could open her purse, he fished a .50
Euro coin from his pocket and pressed it into her hand.
"Here, use this," he said.

"There's something about a legend, isn't there?" she
said, examining the coin.

"Yes. You should throw it with your right hand, over
your left shoulder." He turned her and positioned her
with her back to the fountain. "If you throw one coin,
you will return to Rome, two you will get married, three
you will get divorced."

"I certainly don't need to throw three." As for two…

it was not something she had considered in a long time. She tossed the coin and whirled around to see it splash into the water at Neptune's feet.

"Now it's my turn," Elias said. He reached into his pocket, but she put a hand on his arm to stop him.

"No, I threw your coin. Now you must throw mine."

The coin she gave him was a United States quarter. One with her home state, Pennsylvania, depicted on the front. Fitting, she thought.

Elias's coin, too, landed in the fountain, and they walked on, past the Church of Saints Vincenzo and Anastasio, into yet another square. "Let's stop and rest," Elias said. He gestured toward a sidewalk café. "We can have a drink and a bite to eat."

They sat beneath an umbrella at a lacy iron table and ordered bottled water and antipasto. Elias asked for a bottle of red wine, as well. "We must drink wine at a café in Rome. It will taste better because of the surroundings."

She laughed, pleased at the spark of romance in this otherwise practical businessman. "Thank you for taking me to see the fountain," she said. "It was beautiful."

"I wish I could show you my own country," he said. "Greece is truly the cradle of civilization and there are so many treasures there." His expression clouded. "Unfortunately, there are those who are determined to rape the land of its artifacts and its history. I'm doing everything I can to prevent this. I've established a museum in Athens and contribute to several preservation efforts."

She looked away, reminded of her late husband's possible role in the "rape" Elias decried. "Greed can make people do all sorts of terrible things," she said.

"I did not mean to make you sad." He reached across the table and took her hand. "My pride in my country and my heritage leads me to speak without thinking at times. I apologize."

She nodded, moved both by the tenderness of his touch and the thoughtfulness of his words. She pulled her hand away and composed herself. "Tell me about yourself," she said.

He sat back in his chair. "My family were shipbuilders in Greece," he said. "They were very successful and I inherited the family business, but that eventually translated into a desire to not just build ships but to own them. I started my own cruise line, Argosy Cruises, and last year acquired an American company, Liberty Line. My goal was to outfit a select fleet of ships that would represent the ultimate in luxury. *Alexandra's Dream* is the first such ship."

"And who was Alexandra?" she asked.

"My wife." He acknowledged the waiter who brought them their wine and waited while two glasses were poured. Then he held his glass aloft. "A toast," he said. "To friendship."

"To friendship," she agreed. They touched glasses and she sipped the warm, rich wine. "You're right," she said. "It does taste better."

He nodded, his gaze capturing and holding hers, intense. Yes...there was definitely an attraction there, but she would move slowly. "You were telling me about your wife," she prompted.

"Yes. Alexandra died ten years ago."

He must have loved her very much, to name a ship

after her, but she did not say this. "I know you have one daughter, Katherine. Do you have other children?"

"I have another daughter, Helena." He set aside his wineglass. "Do you have other children besides Ariana?"

"No. Ariana was an only child. And you have a granddaughter, Gemma."

He smiled. "Yes. A beautiful, talented, intelligent young woman. Although, you might say I am prejudiced. Helena's first marriage didn't work out and she's been single awhile now. But she and the captain of *Alexandra's Dream,* Nikolas Pappas, are planning to marry. He's a good man, and good for her."

"I suppose every parent wishes their son or daughter will find love with a partner who will share their life," she said. She blinked past a sudden sting of tears. She wanted so much for Ariana to have love and a family. Would that even be possible now?

Elias leaned forward and took her hand. "I know you are worried about your daughter," he said. "Will you think me foolish if I tell you I think love has a power of its own—that your love is helping to protect her even now?"

Tell that to other parents who have lost children, she thought. But she would not put off his kindness that way. And the idea intrigued her. "I do believe love has a power," she said. "Though I've felt its absence in my life lately."

"I understand your husband passed away earlier this year. Katherine told me the circumstances. I'm very sorry for your loss."

She shook her head. "Derek's death was a shock, as was his arrest before that. But there had been no real love between us, for years." She stared at his hand, still wrapped around hers, fascinated by the dusting of hair across his strong knuckles, by the warmth that seeped into her and by the wealth of comfort and reassurance a simple touch could provide. "I don't know if he was guilty of smuggling antiquities," she said, "but I'm pretty sure he was unfaithful to me, for many years."

"Then, I am sorry, indeed, for that."

He made no move to withdraw his hand, and she was grateful. "Love has been missing from my life for some time," he said. "I have devoted myself to business and to my children's welfare, but, as I grow older, I begin to see that is not enough."

"No, it isn't enough," she said. She had told herself for years that she did not need another person to make her happy, and, though she still believed it was true, she remembered now how rich and satisfying something as simple as a meal and as complex as a life could be when shared.

Their antipasto arrived. Elias cleared his throat and withdrew his hand, though his eyes remained fixed on hers. "I have some time to spend on the ship," he said. "I'd like to spend more of it with you. I know your chief concern is for your daughter, but I hope you will allow me to impose my presence on you a little."

She nodded. "I'd like that very much." Whether anything came of the attraction that sizzled between them, she would return home from this trip with one important gift from him. He had shown her that her heart was not entirely walled off from feeling. That she could risk intimacy and explore desire and perhaps…perhaps… find love again.

WHILE KATHERINE was attempting to come up with a compelling, romantic and even sexy way to lure Charles away from work and everyday worries for an intimate outing with her, June approached her with a special request.

"Albert and I have decided to commemorate our sixtieth anniversary by renewing our vows," she explained when she approached Katherine after lunch the day the ship docked in Civitavecchia.

"Congratulations," Katherine said. "That's a wonderful idea."

"We'd like to do it here, on *Alexandra's Dream*," June told her. "This has become such a special place to us. And I believe ship's captains can perform wedding ceremonies, am I right?"

"Yes, absolutely. When will the ceremony be? Is there anything I can do to help?"

"Our anniversary is Friday," June said. "I know that doesn't give us much time, but I was wondering if you could help plan the celebration? Nothing too elaborate, but I would like it to be nice."

"I'd love to help," Katherine said, with only a brief pang of guilt that this would mean putting off her plans with Charles for a few more days.

"Do you know where on the ship you'd like to have the ceremony?" she asked.

"Yes. I thought perhaps the Court of Dreams," June

beamed. "I always did want to descend a sweeping staircase like that in a beautiful gown."

Katherine nodded. The Court of Dreams, as the ship's main lounge was known, was a tribute to opulence, with an ornate marble staircase with gold railings, Doric columns, a ceiling painted with cherubs and clouds and lighted with fiber-optic stars, and statuary of Greek deities, including Aphrodite, Athena and Poseidon. There was even a concert grand piano where one of the entertainment staff could play the wedding march.

"We can have the wedding in the Court of Dreams," Katherine said, "and the reception in the Garden Terrace." They could turn the rather informal terrace into a semblance of an outdoor garden with the addition of more greenery and flowers and the buffet line could be draped and converted into a serving area for light refreshments. She pulled out a pad of paper and began making notes. "We'll ask the ship's pastry chef to create a wedding cake."

"Maybe something with a Greek temple theme," June said. "All those marble columns and statuaries. So elegant."

Katherine nodded. "Do you have a dress?"

"I have a white evening gown. If you can help me find something for my hair…"

Katherine studied June's mass of white curls. "Let's make an appointment with one of the beauticians in the ship's salon. I'm sure she can come up with something. Some kind of headdress, or a wreath of fresh flowers."

June put her hand over her heart. "My goodness, my heart's fairly racing, this is so exciting."

She had gone very pale and beads of sweat formed on her upper lip. Katherine clutched June's arm, alarmed. "Are you all right? Should I fetch the doctor? Or Albert?"

"Don't be silly. I'm fine." June waved her concern away and took a sip of water. "I was out all morning in the heat, walking too much, I'm sure. And now this excitement." She smiled, some of her color already returning.

Katherine continued to watch her closely, but the renewed strength in June's voice reassured her. "This will be very different from our first wedding, I tell you that," June said.

"Oh? What was your first wedding like?"

"Albert got the license that morning and, on my lunch hour, we went down to the registrar's office and said our vows." She smiled, her eyes taking on a far-away look. "Albert wore his dress uniform. He looked very handsome, I tell you. And I wore a smart suit I'd just finished hemming up the night before. It was coral-colored wool and Albert said I was the prettiest thing he'd ever seen in it."

Katherine could almost see them, two young people, so full of hope. Just as she and Charles had been. What had made the difference for Albert and June? How had their love stayed vibrant for almost sixty years, while she and Charles struggled?

"I reassured Albert I didn't mind saying our vows for the registrar, that neither of us needed the expense and fuss of a big wedding. But, secretly, I did always want the fuss." She smiled at Katherine. "That's what we women dream of from the time we're girls, isn't it?"

Katherine nodded. Her own wedding had been lavish, indeed. Elias had spared no expense for his eldest daughter's nuptials. She had worn a gown from one of England's top designers and had seven attendants. A full dinner and dancing with an orchestra to provide the music had followed, and the young couple had retired to a villa in the South of France for their honeymoon.

"I'm so glad you're going to have the wedding you've always wanted now," she said. "I'll do everything I can to make it wonderful."

"I'm sure you will," June said. "And, after all, it will be wonderful. It's just as I told Albert then—it's the person you're marrying that matters, not the fancy gown and flowers and everything else." She chuckled. "But it will be fun to celebrate in style. And on a cruise ship, no less. It's more than I ever dreamed possible."

Katherine remembered June saying that their children had paid for this trip as an anniversary gift to their parents. "Would you like to arrange for your children to join you for the celebration?" she asked. "We could pick them up in Monte Carlo the day before."

June shook her head. "No, that's all right. They weren't at the first wedding, after all. And I'll have plenty of pictures to show them."

Katherine consulted her list again. "We'll need to make sure the captain is available to officiate, then place an order for flowers with the ship's florist. And discuss food choices with the chef."

June's smile faded. "Is it too much to see to in so little time?" she asked.

Katherine shook her head. "Not at all. You leave everything to me." Planning a renewal ceremony would remind her of the importance of her own wedding vows. Plus, the occasion would be good publicity for the ship, she'd be doing a favor for a friend and it would be good practice for Gemma's eventual wedding.

She resolutely ignored the small voice inside of her that whispered that all the rationalization in the world couldn't hide the fact that she was a coward, using this busyness as an excuse to avoid confronting Charles about the future of their relationship. Though she'd mentioned divorce to her father, she wasn't yet ready to admit that her marriage was over.

CHAPTER NINE

DANTE KEPT ONE EYE on Ariana as he moved toward her, taking cover behind boulders and firing in the direction of her assailant whenever he could get off a shot. One of the Camorra thugs must have seen them near the caves and come after them in a smaller boat or dinghy.

If Sebastian had survived the explosion, he might be able to help them. But Dante had seen no sign of his co-worker. And his first priority now was saving Ariana.

She was trapped between him and the shooter. He hoped she would have enough sense to stay put. If he could get to her, he had a chance of holding off the gunman as they made their way slowly up the coast. If they could reach a better beach and move inland, they might get away.

He was near enough to see her clearly now. Mud streaked her clothing and she looked utterly terrified. The shooter fired off another shot, striking the rock she hid behind. She gave a muffled cry and flattened herself in the sand, waves lapping at her sides, covering her hands. His throat tightened as he remembered her terror of the water earlier—and her courage in facing that fear.

Rage on her behalf made him bold. He started toward her, but was held off by another shot very near him. He couldn't tell if his assailant was merely a poor marksman or purposely missing him, but he didn't want to take a chance.

Ariana crept backward on her hands and knees toward the shore. It was still quite steep here, but a narrow path snaked up through thick brush toward more level ground above. If they could make it there…

Another shot sent Dante diving for cover. Bullets zinged off rocks and splashed in the shallows around him, making it impossible for him to lift his head. Saltwater stung his wounds, but he scarcely felt the pain.

Only Ariana's scream made him risk looking up. He was stunned to see her in the grip of a burly man who held a gun to her temple.

"Throw out your weapon," the man demanded in thickly accented English.

Dante hesitated. The thug shoved the gun hard against Ariana's head. She squeaked, her eyes large and terrified.

"Do it or I will kill the girl!"

Dante tossed the Glock onto the sand in front of him.

"Now you will do exactly as I say. My friend and I are going to take you and the girl for another boat ride."

Dante glanced in the direction of the thug's gaze and saw a yellow Zodiac motoring toward them. The man in the boat looked Greek, as well, Dante thought. The man ran the Zodiac onto the sand and produced a large gun of his own. "Get in," he ordered.

Dante frowned. These men were not Camorra, he

was sure of it. Did that mean *two* groups had been following him and Ariana? And why?

The second thug shoved Ariana into the boat and climbed in after her. Dante tried to catch her eye, to gauge her feelings, but she would not look at him.

The thugs bound their wrists and ankles with twine, then ordered them to lie side by side in the bottom of the boat. Ariana's back was to his, so he had no way of ascertaining her feelings from her expression. But, judging by the stiff set of her shoulders and the slight tremble that ran through her as one of their captors stepped over her to take his seat by the trolling motor that powered the Zodiac, he would say she was terrified.

Dante forced down his own fear and tried to think. As long as they were alive, they had a chance to escape. Not knowing who these men were or what they wanted with the two of them might make the staying alive part prove tricky.

THE NEXT MORNING after confirming that Captain Pappas was, indeed, available to officiate at the renewal of June and Albert's vows, Katherine consulted with the ship's florist about flowers for the ceremony. She was debating the merits of birds of paradise versus roses when her father and Sadie descended the stairs in the Court of Dreams. They walked side by side, heads together, so engrossed in their conversation that they didn't even notice Katherine standing with the florist beneath the stairs.

Katherine frowned as she watched them walk out of

the lounge. Apparently, the attraction she'd sensed between the two of them two days before had not been entirely her imagination. She shrugged off her concern and returned her attention to the florist. "I like all your ideas," she said. "Let's add another arrangement of the stargazer lilies at the base of the stairs. June told me they're a particular favorite of hers."

The flowers agreed upon, Katherine checked Florist off her To Do list and headed for the kitchen to consult with the chef. But, as she exited the Court of Dreams, she almost collided with Charles.

"There you are," he said. "I've been looking for you."

"Walk with me," she said. "I'm on my way to the kitchen."

"Still wearing your wedding planner hat, I see." Charles nodded to the list in her hand.

"With only three days until the ceremony, there's a lot to do," she said. "I want this to be a truly special day for June and Albert."

"They couldn't have picked a better person to see to that."

His flattery pleased her. "You said you were looking for me," she said. "Did you need me for something?"

"I always need you, dear."

His calm voice and placid expression made her wonder at his choice of words. Was he merely being flattering again, or was there deeper meaning there? "Did you need something specific right now?" she prompted.

"I wondered if you wanted to go for a swim with me. Maybe get some sun."

She shook her head. "I can't right now. There's still too much to do."

He nodded, but said nothing further. Was it wrong of her to wish he'd be a little more insistent? "I saw your father and Sadie Bennett just now," he said when they stopped at the door to the kitchen. "They seem to be enjoying each other's company."

She frowned. "I saw them, too."

"Is something wrong? You don't look too pleased with the idea of the two of them together."

"It's nothing." She shook her head. "It's just…I worry because he doesn't know her well. None of us do. What if she's not what she seems?"

"What are you talking about? I thought you liked Sadie."

"I do, but…" She faced him. "Her husband was in prison in America, accused of smuggling antiquities. What if she was involved in that sort of thing with him?"

"There's no reason to think that, is there? Was she accused also?"

"I don't know. She says she wasn't." She studied the list in her hand, not seeing the words there, trying to find a way to voice her own muddled feelings. "I guess I'm just surprised that, after all this time, Dad would show an interest in a woman."

"Why should that surprise you? He's been alone a long time."

"But he was so devoted to my mother. Their marriage was so perfect."

"No marriage is perfect," Charles said.

"Theirs was." Charles had seen her mother and father together—how could he think they'd been anything but soul mates? She studied him. He was so handsome still. So smart and practical, so…unemotional. "If I died, would another woman replace me in your affections so easily?"

"I wouldn't say waiting over ten years was rushing into anything," he said. He took her arm. "Put aside your fretting for a while and come relax with me by the pool. You'll feel better after a swim."

She pulled away from him. "I can't. I really have to talk to the chef about the food for the reception."

"Now who's spending our vacation cruise working?" he asked.

Guilt stabbed at her, and she studied the list again. Only a few things were checked off. "I promised June I'd take care of everything. I can't let her down."

"All right." Charles nodded, his face as impassive as ever. If he was annoyed with her, he didn't let it show. Somehow, his lack of anger made her feel even worse. "I'll be by the pool when you're done," he said.

"I'll be quick as I can, I promise." If she hurried, she could join him in another couple of hours. They'd still be able to salvage most of the day.

He left her and she opened the door to the kitchen. Life was always like this—all the duties and details getting in the way of affection. Jobs, children and other obligations stole so much of the time they had once spent together.

Maybe the reason June and Albert and her parents had such enduring marriages was that they hadn't had so many claims on their time. They hadn't been pulled in so many directions, until they were literally pulled apart.

She glanced at the list again. She could talk to the entertainment staff tomorrow. That should shave an hour off her time away from Charles.

He had said she was a person who made things happen. It was time she turned those skills to her marriage. She would make things work with Charles.

And, if they didn't, she'd know she had done everything she could before she walked away.

AN HOUR AND A HALF after she and Charles parted, Katherine had settled on a menu for the reception and returned to her rooms and changed into her bathing suit. She was on her way to the pool to join Charles when Tom flagged her down. "Katherine, wait up!" he called.

She stopped in the hallway outside the elevators and waited for him to reach her. "How have you been?" he asked, jogging up to her. He was in uniform again, tanned and handsome as ever.

"Busy," she said. "I'm helping a couple put together a vows renewals ceremony to celebrate their sixtieth wedding anniversary."

"I guess that's what happens when you're the boss's daughter," he said. "You end up working even when you're on vacation."

"I volunteered to help. I'm enjoying it, really." And she *had* enjoyed the planning and preparations. She excelled at this kind of organizational task, and the hours she'd been occupied with this had been hours she hadn't spent fretting over her marriage or her father or the missing Ariana Bennett. "What have you been doing besides working?" she asked. "Did you get a chance to see any sites in Rome?"

"A few. But it wasn't the same without you there." His tone was casual, but his eyes searched hers, a more serious message in that intense gaze.

Was the corridor always this uncomfortably warm? Or was it only because Tom was standing so close? She looked away, though she could still feel his gaze, like a physical caress. She felt exposed and vulnerable, aware of the bikini under her gauzy cover-up. The suit was a daring style for her, of a coppery-black, shimmery fabric, and not a great deal of it.

"You look great," Tom said, as if reading her thoughts. "I guarantee no man will be looking at anyone else when you show up at the pool."

She pulled the cover-up more closely around her. "I'm sure all the twentysomethings I see hanging out there have nothing to worry about."

"And I say a real man wouldn't look twice at them when a woman like you was around." He moved closer, one hand braced against the wall beside her. "I really enjoyed the time we spent together the other day," he said.

She *should* say something now about needing to get to Charles. Remind Tom that she was married. Step away and let him know his implied intimacy wasn't welcome.

She should do all these things, but, when she opened

her mouth, what came out was "I enjoyed it, too." No lie there. Tom was the kind of man who made any woman feel young and sexy and desirable. Intense and brash, he would no doubt argue as passionately as he would make love.

The thought made her blush. Where had that come from? She had no intention of learning whether Tom was a passionate lover or not…though she sensed, if she raised the possibility of an affair, he would not find the idea disagreeable.

That she could even consider such a thing didn't say much for the current state of her marriage. The knowledge only confused her more. "I have to go," she said. "Charles is waiting for me."

"He's a lucky man." Tom stepped back, giving her room to pass. "I hope he knows it."

Did Charles consider himself lucky? Or did he consider the question at all? Both of them had spent so many years taking their marriage—and each other—for granted.

Yes, Charles was placid and dispassionate, but he hadn't always been that way. In their younger years, he'd impressed her with his drive and, yes, his *passion.* Had age stolen that edge from him, or merely familiarity and comfort?

Their marriage was anything but comfortable now, at least for her. She glanced over her shoulder and saw Tom still watching her. He caught her eye now and winked, an openly sexy look that sent heat curling through her. She couldn't deny the pleasure in having a man look at her that way. Or the disappointment that came with thinking that her husband might never look at her that way again.

If he didn't, what would she do then? Tom had made it plain he was interested in her. Whatever happened next was up to her. It was both a powerful and a paralyzing position to be in.

CHARLES RETIRED to the pool to read and wait for Katherine. Though he was disappointed to be here alone, he wasn't surprised she'd agreed to help with June and Albert's ceremony. It was so typical of her to go out of her way to help someone else. Her compassion was one of the things he loved most about her.

He'd been surprised when, four years ago, she'd approached him with the idea of starting her own public relations firm. True, she had a marketing degree and had spent years using her skills to help various charities, with great success. In the early days of their marriage, she'd sometimes talked of going to work for one of the large marketing firms in London, but Gemma had arrived quickly and Katherine had devoted herself to caring for their child. They'd hoped for more children to follow and had struggled with disappointment for several years before accepting the reality that another pregnancy was not to be.

Gemma and charity work had satisfied Katherine's aspirations for many years. Charles worked hard and built his own career. After several years employed by others, he opened his own firm, which quickly grew. It had been an exciting time of long hours and a lot of travel. Knowing Katherine was always there, waiting at home, had kept him going.

But he hadn't hesitated when she'd suggested opening her own business. He'd encouraged her every way he could and wasn't surprised she'd been an immediate success.

The thing about Katherine that set her apart from every other PR firm out there was the same compassion that had made her such a great advocate for every charitable cause for which she'd volunteered. She saw public relations as more of a calling than a job and put everything she had into helping people build a business or promote a project as if it—and they—were the most important things in the world to her at that moment.

But, he had to admit, he missed his wife being there for him, one hundred percent of the time. For the first time, he realized how lonely it must have been for her, when he was traveling the world, while she remained at home with Gemma. She had never complained, but, now that he was sometimes the one waiting for her to return from visiting a client, he felt a little guilty about all he'd put her through.

But the great thing about Katherine was that she always understood him. Things were hectic for them both now, but life would slow down soon enough and they'd be able to pick up where they'd left off, finding time once more for long conversations and slow love-making—things they had not had much opportunity for so far this trip.

He glanced away from the pool and saw a woman in a black bikini walking toward him. She had the kind of curves that had every man on the deck turning his head to stare. He felt his own heartbeat quicken, proving that at forty-one he still wasn't immune to the sight of a sexy woman.

Only when the woman was closer did he realize he was staring at his own wife. The suit was obviously new—more daring that anything she usually wore. And she looked good in it. Really good. Pride surged through him at the thought that this gorgeous woman was his wife. He sat up and smiled at her. "I think every man here is envious of me right this minute," he said.

She flushed and pretended not to understand. "I don't know what you're talking about."

"You look amazing." He rose and kissed her and continued to hold her hand as they sat on loungers, side by side. He was ready to suggest they head straight for their rooms, but thought better of it. It might be nice to enjoy admiring her in that bikini a while longer. And there was a lot to be said for anticipation.

"Thanks," she said, and lay back on the lounger.

"Did you get everything done you needed to do?" he asked.

"Most of it. It's going to be a beautiful ceremony. I think they'll be pleased."

"June and Albert don't strike me as people who are difficult to please."

"Do you think that's the secret to their successful marriage?" she asked. "That neither of them is overly particular?"

He laughed. "I wouldn't put it that way. Maybe a better word is *easygoing*. They don't strike me as the types to worry about petty things."

She frowned. "You think I worry too much."

He took her hand and squeezed it. "You do, but that's not what I meant. I was thinking that June and Albert are people who live in the moment. They don't fret about the past or the future."

She nodded, though her smile had not returned. "That's easier said than done for some of us." She closed her eyes. "I think what I want to do right this moment is relax and enjoy the sun."

"That sounds like a plan. And I'm going to enjoy watching you in that amazing swimsuit."

Her smile returned. "You think this suit is amazing?"

"The suit...and the woman in it."

Her smiled broadened. "Flatterer." But she sounded pleased. He smiled to himself. What had he said? The old closeness was still there, waiting to resurface. All they had to do was be patient and let it happen.

THE NEPTUNE BALL was an event viewed as the highlight of the cruise for many passengers on *Alexandra's Dream*. A chance to parade their most exquisite finery and dance until the wee hours, it was an event many had looked forward to all week.

Sadie was not one of these. She'd planned to spend the evening in her cabin, away from the music and wine and all the reminders of the romance lacking in her life.

Until Elias had asked her if she would be attending. She didn't even hesitate to answer. "I'll be there if you will."

"I wouldn't miss it," he'd said, with a smile that had warmed her to her toes.

So here she was now, in a gown purchased only this

morning in the ship's boutique, arm in arm with a man who made her heart race and her thoughts whirl. She was dimly aware of curious looks from the other dancers and whispers when they passed. Most people knew that Elias was the owner of *Alexandra's Dream.* They no doubt wondered what he was doing with a nobody like her. But, when he looked into her eyes, she forgot all about them. She hadn't felt this wonderful—this *alive*—in years.

If only Ariana were safe and well, life would be perfect.

The music ended and he escorted her to the table they shared alongside the dance floor. "I have some news for you," he said, pulling out her chair for her. "But I wanted you to be sitting down when I told you."

All the breath rushed out of her at his words and she felt dizzy. "Ariana?" she gasped.

"As far as I know, she's fine." He scooted his own chair closer and took her hand. "I had word from the new investigator I hired. He's turned up evidence that a worker at the diggings in Paestum disappeared about the same time Ariana did. And she was seen talking with him at the dig site that morning."

She could breathe again, though her heart skipped erratically. She squeezed Elias's hand so hard her fingers hurt, desperate to hold on to any scrap of hope he might give her. "Do they know the man's name? Where he's from? What he's like?"

"Only a first name. Dante. The other workers said he's not local, that he hadn't been with them long. They don't know where he's from. As for what he's like…"

He shrugged. "These workers are a pretty rough lot. I would imagine he's the same."

By *rough* did he mean uneducated and unpolished— or coarse and even cruel? She was afraid to ask. "Do they think Ariana is with him?"

"No one knows," Elias said. "Did Ariana ever mention anyone like him to you? Anyone named Dante, or an Italian man she was seeing?"

Sadie shook her head. "She never said anything like that. She never mentioned anyone but friends here on the ship." The rush of hope his initial words had brought was receding, replaced by a deeper despair. If Ariana was with this "rough man" no one knew anything about, what was she doing? Was she safe? Or was she trapped somewhere, or hurt, or...

Elias grasped her shoulders. "I can see in your eyes you're thinking the worst," he said. "Don't do it. We're going to keep looking. Now that we have this clue to help, we're that much closer to finding her. Here, drink this."

She sipped from the glass of champagne he handed her. "You're right," she said. "And thank you." She offered him a weak smile. "I don't know what I'd do without you right now."

"I'm glad you don't have to find out."

Applause from the dance floor distracted them. They turned to see June and Albert dancing an exuberant jitterbug. Elias laughed. "Those two are amazing," he said. "I hope I have half that much fun at their age."

"Or half that much energy," Sadie added as Albert bent June back over his arm and kissed her soundly.

She and Elias joined in the applause as the song ended. "Would you like to dance some more?" he asked as the next song began.

She shook her head. "Not yet. I want to sit and watch for a while." A fascinating spectacle whirled by their seat along the dance floor—women in designer gowns both elegant and outrageous, men as polished as their partners, dancers both accomplished and less so, but everyone appearing to enjoy themselves immensely.

Katherine and her husband, Charles, danced by. Katherine wore a form fitting, teal-colored gown shot through with silver thread, silvery ribbon woven through her piled up hair. "Katherine looks lovely tonight," Sadie said. "You must be so proud of her."

"I am. But she works too hard." He gave a rueful smile. "She takes after me, I'm afraid."

"That's not so bad, is it?"

"When I was younger I would have said no, but now…" He shook his head. "I suppose life makes one more philosophical. Now I see what all those hours at work cost me in time I could have spent with my family. Time I'll never get back." He glanced at her. "I don't want Katherine and Charles to make the mistakes I did."

Was he thinking of time he wished he'd spent with his wife, now that she was gone? Or the youth they all had spent so unthinkingly? "We all wish our children could avoid ever being hurt," she said. "But there are some lessons everyone has to learn for themselves."

He nodded. "I wish Katherine wasn't always so practical."

"You mean, she hasn't inherited your bent for romance?" she teased.

He took her hand and leaned in close, his voice a low rumble that made her tremble with desire. "Apparently not."

She closed her eyes, sure he would kiss her, anticipating the feel of his lips on her own, when shouts from the dance floor intruded.

Elias released her hand and straightened. Sadie opened her eyes and, through a gap in the crowd, saw people gathered around a woman who was prostrate on the dance floor.

"It's June Westcott," Elias said, standing.

Sadie hurried after him. They arrived in time to see Albert and two others helping June to her feet. "I'm fine," June pleaded, waving them away. "I got too hot, that's all." She clung to her husband's arm, looking pale and weak. "I'll be fine as soon as I sit and rest a minute."

"Are you sure you don't want me to call a doctor?" Elias asked.

"Thank you, but I'll be fine." June smiled. "I'll go to my room now and try to remember to act my age in the future."

Chuckles greeted this remark and she was allowed to leave.

Elias turned to Sadie, his smile as full of regret as she felt. "I don't know about acting our age, but would you like to dance?"

She moved into his arms—the best place she could think of to be. "I'd love to."

CHAPTER TEN

"I HOPE JUNE IS ALL RIGHT," Katherine said, watching over Charles's shoulder as Albert escorted his wife from the ballroom.

"I'm not surprised she's tired after the way she was dancing." Charles pulled Katherine closer and guided her expertly around the dance floor.

"She should be more careful," Katherine said. "She looked very pale just now, I thought."

"I'm sure she's taken good care of herself so far, to have lived this long."

She nodded. "I know I worry too much." She smiled. "I guess you could say it's a habit I picked up the day I found out I was pregnant with Gemma, and I haven't been able to let go of it since."

"I'm sure there are worse habits a person could have."

At least he hadn't tried to talk her out of worrying.

They passed her father and Sadie, who were dancing close. They were talking and laughing, their attention focused on one another with the air of two people who had forgotten another world even existed.

"Elias looks as if he's enjoying himself," Charles said.

"Yes, he does." She couldn't remember when she'd seen her father looking so well.

"Sadie's a beautiful woman," Charles said. "I'm certainly no expert, but she doesn't strike me as a gold digger or con artist or anything other than the widow and worried mother she says she is."

Katherine nodded. "I'm sure you're right. And, if I didn't know what I do about her late husband, or even if my father had more experience dating, I might be more comfortable with the situation."

Charles squeezed her hand. "I don't think your mother would disapprove. I doubt she'd want your father to spend the rest of his life alone and, don't you think, if she was still alive, she and Sadie would be friends?"

"I hadn't thought of that." Sadie was exactly the sort of woman her mother would have befriended. "As much as Mom loved Dad, I can't imagine she'd have wanted him to be alone." She smiled up at him. Charles's amazingly even temperament and logical mind might frustrate her at times, but, at this moment, she was very grateful for his calming presence. "Thank you," she said. "Sometimes I guess I need the obvious pointed out to me."

"You're a smart woman. You'd have figured it out sooner or later."

The praise warmed her. Charles was not one to hand out idle compliments. Sometimes, she wished he was more generous with his flattery, but, at times like these, she valued his praise more because of its scarcity.

The song finished and they started back toward their

table when Tom intercepted her. Resplendent in his dazzling white dress uniform, he glanced at Charles, then made a formal bow to Katherine. "May I have the honor of this dance?" he asked.

His request and his overly formal manner, flustered her. "I, well…" She looked at Charles, who was scowling at Tom with obvious dislike. But, when he saw Katherine watching him, he resumed his normally placid expression.

"Don't let me stop you," he said.

Before she could say more, Tom took her hand and pulled her toward the dance floor. She went with him, confused by Charles's reaction. If he didn't like Tom—if he clearly didn't want her to dance with him—why didn't he say something? Yes, the decision was ultimately hers, but she would have appreciated a bit more possessiveness on his part—some show that he wanted to keep her to himself.

But, of course, Charles was much too civilized and correct for anything like that. She glanced over her shoulder and saw that he was still standing on the edge of the dance floor, brow furrowed, his expression unreadable.

Tom pulled her into his arms, too close for propriety. She drew away from him to a more proper distance. He grinned. "Can't blame a man for trying, can you?" He squeezed her right hand. "You're looking especially beautiful tonight, Katherine. I haven't been able to take my eyes off you."

The words should have pleased her, so why did she get the feeling they were the kind of thing he might say to any dance partner? It wouldn't surprise her to learn that he *had* said much the same thing to every woman he'd danced with tonight.

"How are you enjoying the cruise?" Tom asked.

The same kind of innocuous small talk he would make with any other passenger. She relaxed. Maybe she'd mistaken his natural bent to flirtation for real attraction.

"I'm enjoying the cruise," she said lightly. "It's nice to be a passenger for a change."

"But you've been busy, haven't you?" He looked down at her, his gaze as overly familiar as his embrace had been. "Planning a wedding and things like that."

"It's a vows renewal ceremony, but, yes, it's taken up some of my time. I was happy to do it."

"It's nice that you have other things to keep you busy, with Charles so involved in his work."

His voice had a nasty edge she didn't like. She felt compelled to defend her husband. "Charles has had a few business things to see to, but it's not as if he's working all the time."

"Then, why do I see you alone so much of the time?" He leaned closer, his voice low. "If I had more free time, I'd certainly spend it with you."

More flirtation, or real interest? She no longer wanted to know. His attentions made her uncomfortable, but whether that was because she didn't want them—or because she wanted them too much—she didn't care to examine. She changed the subject.

"When we were in Kusadasi, you volunteered to ask

Giorgio Tzekas about Ariana Bennett," she said. "Did you talk to him?"

"I did." He shrugged. "He didn't tell me anything new."

His dismissal of her question annoyed her. "What did he say, *exactly?*"

Tom frowned. "What difference does it make?" He pulled her closer. "I'd much rather talk about you. About us."

Again, she pulled away from him, using more force this time. She could have refused to dance with him altogether, but she didn't want to make a scene. And she was truly interested in finding out what Giorgio had told him. "I want to know about Ariana," she said. "What did Giorgio say?"

"That she was a tease. That she led him on, then shut him out. His words weren't that polite, but that's the gist of it."

She could imagine the kind of words Giorgio would have used. The man could be very crude. He, no doubt, said similar things about her. "Does he have any idea why she left the ship in Naples?"

"He thinks she was probably snooping where she didn't belong and got what she deserved."

His words—and the casual way in which they were delivered—chilled her. "You…you sound as if you agree with him," she stammered.

He shrugged. "Maybe I do." He tried to pull her closer. "I really don't care about Ariana Bennett. I'd much rather talk about you."

She struggled to keep a respectable distance between them. "Charles is watching," she murmured.

"I don't care if he is," Tom said, his voice belliger-
ent. "If you were my wife, I wouldn't allow you to
dance with anyone else."

"Charles doesn't try to control me that way," she
said.

"He doesn't try—or he doesn't care?"

She stopped dancing and stumbled back from him.

"What's wrong?" he asked, trying to pull her to
him once more.

"I…I'm suddenly not feeling very well," she said.
She hurried to the edge of the dance floor and started
toward the ladies' room. She needed a few moments to
collect herself before she faced Charles.

In the ladies' room, she applied a damp towel to
her throat and studied her face in the mirror. Thanks to
an excellent colorist, her hair was still a soft shade of
brown with blond highlights. But a few fine lines across
her forehead and around her eyes betrayed the fact
that she was not as young as she had once been. She
could honestly say she was attractive, but not gorgeous.
So why all this attention from Tom? Not to mention
Giorgio? Was she giving off vibes that she was available?

Or had someone spread gossip among the ship's
crew that she and Charles were having problems? She
couldn't imagine who might do such a thing, but her
father had been in the cruise industry long enough for
her to know that shipboard life was claustrophobic and
anything but private. And, like the old game of tele-
phone, some bit of gossip whispered to one person
could grow into an entirely different rumor by the time
it had finished making the rounds.

Worse, had *Charles* said something to make people believe he no longer cared? The thought made her sick to her stomach. She leaned against the sink, trying to collect herself. She couldn't believe Charles no longer cared. Maybe they had grown apart, but he would have told her if he no longer had any feelings for her, wouldn't he?

In any case, she was determined to avoid Tom and focus on Charles from now on. She had taken this trip in order to strengthen her marriage, so that was exactly what she would devote herself to doing.

She freshened her lipstick and smoothed her hair, then exited the restroom, prepared to be sparkling and vivacious—the perfect evening's date.

But she had not gone far when a hand snaked out and pulled her into a secluded alcove. A hand over her mouth kept her from crying out. Heart hammering in her chest, she fought against her attacker, but strong arms held her firm.

"Will you be still?" a familiar voice hissed in her ear. "I'm not going to hurt you. Unless I have to."

She froze, then turned her head to stare at Giorgio. "Are you going to be quiet?" he asked. "I only want to talk to you."

She nodded, though she debated screaming as soon as he took his hand from her mouth. Only the embarrassment she knew she'd suffer if she attracted attention to the two of them kept her silent. "I thought I told you not to come near me again," she said when he uncovered her mouth. "Ever!"

"I don't take orders from you," he said. Exactly like

some B-grade movie villain. She wondered if Giorgio saw himself playing some kind of role—if his twisted mind lived a fantasy, rather than the drabness of everyday life.

"What do you want?" she asked, straightening her gown where he'd rumpled it.

"I saw you dancing with Tom just now," he said, his sneering smile once more in place.

"That's generally what people do at a dance," she said. His threats were getting tiresome. She had half a mind to go to Charles and tell him everything. Then she'd tell her father and her Giorgio problems would be over.

"I wonder what your daughter would think about her mother throwing herself at a handsome young officer," Giorgio said. "Do you think she'd be upset?"

A red haze clouded Katherine's vision. "You leave Gemma out of this," she said, her hands curled into fists.

Giorgio was unmoved by her anger. "A very pretty girl, Gemma. Very sweet and innocent. I have her e-mail, you know."

"You've e-mailed Gemma?" The idea made her queasy. Gemma had never mentioned such a correspondence, but perhaps she wouldn't. She imagined how Giorgio might appear to a young girl like Gemma. Someone who didn't know his history. She might think him handsome, dashing even. She might be flattered by his attention... She shook her head. Gemma was much more intelligent than that. And she was a good judge of people. She would see through Giorgio's act and laugh at any attempt he might make to ingratiate himself with her.

"I haven't yet, but I could," he said. "I could tell her about all her mother's embarrassing actions, carrying on with the handsome young chief engineer, right under her father's nose."

"There is no carrying on."

"But she won't know that, will she?"

Anger was a hard knot in her chest. She wanted to tell Giorgio to go to hell. She wanted to run straight to her father and demand that he put the first officer off the ship immediately. But she had no doubt Giorgio would carry out his threat and send Gemma his distorted stories.

Gemma might not believe them, but, even then, the damage would be done. A little more distance would grow between them, a little more erosion of trust.

And Charles—Charles would be hurt by such accusations, too, no matter that they were lies. "What do you want from me?" she asked.

"Continue to keep quiet. I keep my job. You keep your life the way you want it." He spread his hands, palms out. "Very simple."

"Leave me alone and I won't have any reason to say anything to anyone," she said. "I'll pretend I never knew you—and I ask you to do the same."

He glared at her, as if debating further threats. But he must have seen the determination in her eyes; she wouldn't let him bully her. At last, he nodded. "Then, we have an agreement." He stepped aside. "Say hello to Charles for me."

She made her way blindly to her table, feeling dizzy and sick with rage. The man was odious. A rush of sympathy for Ariana Bennett swept over her. Could it be she had left the ship in Naples in order to escape Giorgio's persistent attentions? But, if that were so, why hadn't she at least contacted her mother?

When she approached their table, Charles was deep in conversation with his friend Gideon, the ship's chief security officer. When she groped for her chair, he stood. "Katherine, are you all right?" he asked. "You look pale."

"I...I must have gotten a little too warm." She sank into a chair and smoothed her hands down her dress. "I'll be all right in a moment."

"I'll get you a glass of water," Gideon offered, and left them.

Charles moved his chair closer to hers. "Did something happen out there?" he asked. "Did Tom say something to upset you?"

Tom. She'd almost forgotten about Tom. "We were talking about Ariana Bennett," she said, forcing her mind away from its attempts to replay the scene with Giorgio.

Charles frowned. "Why were you discussing Ariana?"

"When Tom and I saw Sadie Bennett, that afternoon in Kusadasi, he promised to talk to Giorgio Tzekas and ask if he had any idea what happened to Ariana."

"I thought the rumors that Ms. Bennett and Tzekas were involved were false."

"They were, but Giorgio did spend a lot of time

hanging around Ariana, so I thought it might be worth talking to him."

"What did Tzekas tell Tom?"

"He said Ariana was probably snooping where she shouldn't be and got what she deserved." She shuddered. "I can't help thinking how I'd feel if Gemma was in Ariana's situation. I hope for Sadie's sake that Giorgio is wrong."

Charles took her hand and squeezed it. "The girl rejected Giorgio and wounded his overblown ego," he said. "He's saying nasty things about her out of spite, not out of any real knowledge, I'm sure."

She nodded. Charles had sized up Giorgio correctly, though he could have no idea how dangerously arrogant the man was.

Gideon returned with the water. "Are you feeling better?" he asked.

"Yes, better, thank you." She accepted the water and took a sip. "I'll be fine when I've rested a bit."

"Then, I'll leave you two and get back to mingling."

When they were alone again, Charles looked out over the dance floor. "Tom certainly seems taken with you."

An icy chill swept over her. Had Giorgio said something to Charles already? "Tom flirts with every woman," she said, struggling to keep her voice from shaking. "He doesn't mean anything by it."

"I'm not surprised he's singled you out." Charles turned his attention back to her. "You're a smart, accomplished, beautiful woman. Did I tell you how much I liked the bikini you wore this afternoon?"

So many compliments from her husband in one evening made her blush. "You may have mentioned it once or twice." Truthfully, Charles had been particularly attentive this afternoon, behavior that had added to her confusion over her feelings for Tom. She wondered if Charles had sensed her interest in the engineer, or if something else had prompted the change in behavior.

"I'm almost finished the arrangements for June and Albert's ceremony," she said.

"Does this mean you'll be able to relax now?" he asked.

"It does." She leaned closer to him. "Thank you for being so patient. Tomorrow, I want us to take a day just for ourselves."

He slid his hand down her thigh, definite interest in the blue depths of his eyes. "I like the idea."

"We'll be in Monaco," she said. "Do you remember when we went there on our honeymoon?"

"Mmm. I do. We rented that Alfa Romeo and drove along the coast."

"We can do that again if you like. Or visit the beach. Or whatever, as long as we're together. Alone." She kissed his cheek. "We won't tell anyone where we're going. Not my father or your office or anyone."

"I'm liking this idea better and better." He caressed her thigh and gave her a genuinely heated look. "What do you say we go back to the room and start reliving the honeymoon early?"

Her breath caught, and a nervous laugh escaped, like effervescence rushing from a newly opened bottle of champagne. "That sounds like a wonderful idea."

So maybe the passion wasn't gone entirely. Or maybe her encounter with Tom had reminded her there was more than one way to capture a man's interest.

CHAPTER ELEVEN

IN THE ELEVATOR on the way to their room, Katherine leaned back against Charles as he wrapped his arms around her waist. She closed her eyes and rubbed up against him suggestively, but he remained still. He wasn't the type to make out in an elevator, even one in which they were the only passengers. Though, most of the time, she appreciated his maturity and responsibility, there were moments when she wished he was a little wilder. She longed to be swept up in uncontrollable passion—to be a woman a man couldn't wait to have.

Once behind the locked door of their penthouse, however, Charles became more passionate. He pulled her tightly against him and kissed her until she was breathless. "You are amazing," he said, and smoothed his hands down her back to cradle her bottom.

In that moment, she *felt* amazing, dizzy with passion in a way she had not been since the early days of their marriage, when they had spent hours of every week in bed, unable to get enough of each other.

She had blamed their recent lackluster sex life on age and waning hormones and the boredom of familiarity that was the inevitable fallout of any long marriage. But the tingling in her senses and fevered urgency of her need tonight made her believe she'd been wrong. Maybe the only thing amiss with their sex life lately was a lack of effort to make it more exciting.

Cool air rushed across her back as Charles lowered the zipper on her dress. She tugged at his tie, the silk sliding through her fingers, reminding her of unwrapping a wonderful present.

He pulled the dress from her shoulders, his warm hands caressing her naked back, sending flutters of arousal all through her. She hurried to slip off his tie, then began undoing the buttons of his shirt. When his chest was naked she pressed her lips to the hard curve of muscle over his heart and ran her hands over his still-flat stomach.

He made a growling sound low in his throat and shoved her dress to her waist, then to the floor, and quickly unfastened her bra, freeing her breasts, which he covered with his hands, squeezing gently. "You're beautiful," he said. Words he'd said hundreds of times before whenever she faced him naked, yet, she never doubted the sincerity of the sentiment. She wondered if he saw her as she was now, softened and rounded with age, or, if in his eyes, she was always the firm and ripe nineteen-year-old who had faced him their first time together.

She smiled at the thought that love could have this special kind of blindness. After all, when she looked at him, she saw not his flaws, but the things about him that had always attracted her—the firm jut of his jaw, his strong shoulders and arms, his flat stomach and muscular thighs. Even if he no longer had the chiseled frame of a twenty-year-old, her body still had that memory to fuel her desire.

They moved to the bed, taking off the rest of their clothes on the way. She knelt on the bed and Charles stood facing her, kissing her deeply, lingering in their pleasure. She threaded her fingers through his hair and leaned back, guiding his mouth to her breasts. This was what she loved, this slow building of sensation until it was almost more than she could bear.

She moaned, her fingers digging into his shoulders, imagining his need growing as great as hers. She smiled, picturing him behind her closed eyelids, his legs apart, braced, his hand clutching her hips, his mouth seeking her other breast. His long legs, tight buttocks, straight back, each vertebrae defined, wiry arms, dark hair curling against his collar…

She gasped and opened her eyes, stunned by the picture her imagination had conjured. The man she had fantasized was not Charles, but Tom Diamantopoulos.

Charles groaned and pulled her closer, apparently mistaking her gasp for a sign of enthusiasm. He urged her down onto the bed and moved to lie beside her. She tried to regain her focus on him, on this time for them to be together, but, whenever she closed her eyes, she saw Tom again, or at least the way she imagined he would look naked.

"Is something wrong?" Charles leaned back and looked at her.

"Wrong? No. Why would you think that?" She smoothed her hand down the sheets, avoiding his gaze.

"You seem distracted."

"I'm just getting comfortable on the bed." She smiled and reached for him. "Now where were we?"

He grinned and kissed her. She arched against him, doing her best to act out an enthusiasm she did not feel. She knew all the moves to make—where to put her hand, when to shift to allow deeper access, what noises to make to encourage him. But while her body acted, her mind raced. She was in bed with her husband, a wonderful man. What was she doing fantasizing about a younger man who had only flirted with her? What was wrong with her?

She rolled to her back, bringing Charles on top of her. He knelt between her legs and she reached to guide him into her, all the while smiling, hoping in the grip of desire he would not sense that her own ardor had faded. As he entered her, she lay back and closed her eyes once more.

She was tempted to abandon herself to her fantasies of Tom—to allow the idea of making love to another man fuel her desire and enhance this moment with Charles. But such thoughts felt like the worst sort of betrayal. She was ashamed to even think them, not to mention her fear that she might accidentally call out Tom's name in the throes of passion. What would Charles think then?

What else *could* he think? She'd be accused of cheating on her husband with the chief engineer, when all she'd done so far was engage in a little mild flirtation.

And some not-so-mild fantasizing.

She closed her eyes and debated faking an orgasm,

but that felt like a betrayal, also. A white lie, true, but still a lie.

Then again, even being here now, pretending to desire her husband, to want to be in his arms when all she felt was empty, was a kind of lie.

In the end, she sensed that Charles was waiting for her to come first, so she pretended to find release in order that he might surrender to his own climax. When he withdrew and lay down beside her once more, she pulled away and retreated to the bathroom, near tears.

She turned the water on full blast so he wouldn't hear her sobbing and pressed a wet washrag to her face, panic fueling her tears. If June was right, that a vibrant sexual relationship was the key to a lasting marriage, then she and Charles were in big trouble.

THE MORNING AFTER THE BALL, when the ship was due to anchor in the harbor at Monte Carlo, Sadie stood before the lighted glass case in the ship's library and studied the artifacts displayed there. A vase labeled as a container for olive oil presented to the victor in Greek athletic competitions glowed in tones of gold and ebony. A bust of Aphrodite stared back at her, serene and beautiful through the ages. A small gold tablet made her think of the kings and queens who must have held it.

Of course, all of these items were reproductions, but they made Sadie think of the genuine artifacts that had fascinated collectors for centuries. Items for which great wealth had been spent and whole lives squandered.

She could make the argument that artifacts like these had almost ruined her life. First, they had taken her husband away from her for long periods of time. His job as a museum curator required him to travel to search for new acquisitions for the museum's collection. And, even when he was home, he was more often than not preoccupied with researching the history of various items both online and in books.

Later, if the charges against Derek were to be believed, his passion for antiquities had turned into obsession, or perhaps only a way to feed his greed. His arrest and the subsequent publicity had destroyed his reputation and Sadie's, as well. Privacy had become a thing of the past and people she had counted as friends had deserted her.

And now, such treasures may have taken her daughter from her, as well. Ariana had been seen at the dig site in Paestum. Had she gone there because she'd found something that linked that particular site to Derek's activities? Or had her visit been a way for her to feel closer to her father? Was it merely a coincidence that she'd been seen speaking to this Dante person shortly before she disappeared, or did something link them?

Sadie felt no closer to finding Ariana, and, on that count, the cruise might be declared a loss. But, though she had boarded *Alexandra's Dream* to search for her daughter, Sadie could admit she'd also welcomed the chance to get away—to escape the stares and whispers of her neighbors and acquaintances.

Here, she had begun to feel like her old self again. She'd made new friends and rediscovered the joy of something as simple as a conversation with someone who wasn't interrogating or judging her.

And then there was Elias, perhaps the greatest gift—and the most unexpected—of this entire venture. Last night on the dance floor she'd been certain he'd felt the pull of attraction between them.

She'd thought herself too wounded by the hurts of the past to allow herself to love again, but Elias had shown her how wrong she'd been.

She focused on a vase decorated with a depiction of two lovers and dared to hope she might one day find love again.

The door to the library opened and Father Connelly entered. "Mrs. Bennett," he said. "I hope I'm not disturbing you."

"Of course not, Father." She stood and turned to greet him.

"I see you've been admiring my collection of replicas," he said, joining her in front of the display case.

"Yes. You have some nice examples."

"You must attend my lecture sometime and learn more about them," he said. "Then again, as the widow of a museum curator, you probably already know everything I have to say."

She frowned. "How did you know that my husband was a museum curator?"

He blinked. "You must have told me."

She shook her head. "I'm sure I didn't." She talked about Derek to very few people.

"Then, your daughter must have mentioned it." He nodded. "Yes, I'm sure she did."

No doubt Ariana had. She was proud of her father and loved to talk about his work. "I'm afraid I didn't share my husband's interest in artifacts," Sadie said. "Nor did he talk much about his work when he was at home." In retrospect, she could see they had seldom talked of anything that wasn't related to Ariana or the house or the minutiae of everyday life. They had never discussed feelings or hopes or dreams or anything of real importance to a relationship.

"Didn't he?" Father Connelly shrugged. "Well, I suppose he knew you weren't interested." He turned to the case. "The jewelry usually attracts the women who attend my lectures. That, and the decorative objects like the vase. Men tend to focus on the coins and the dagger—money and weapons." He glanced at her. "I find that interesting, don't you?"

According to the information in the schedule of activities for *Alexandra's Dream,* Father Connelly was a fellow of the Society for American Archaeology and a former associate of the Vatican's Etruscan Museum. She had heard he now taught at a boys' school somewhere in the Midwest. "Father, did you know my husband?" she asked.

He started, though he tried to mask his obvious alarm by looking away. "Your husband? Why would I know him?"

"You share his interest in Greco-Roman artifacts," she said. "And an interest in teaching. I'm sure if Derek hadn't been a museum curator, he would have been a professor." If only he had taken that route instead of going to work for the museum. Maybe even now he'd be alive and lecturing on a cruise ship, like Father Connelly.

The priest shook his head. "No, I did not know him."

He continued to avoid her gaze, running his thumb back and forth across the lock on the display cabinet. If he had been anything but a priest, she might have thought he was lying to her, or at least not revealing the entire truth. "I thought maybe your paths had crossed at some time," she said. "After all, they say it's a small world, and the world of antiquities is even smaller."

He bowed his head for a long moment, almost as if in prayer, though she suspected he was merely thinking. When he lifted it again and met her gaze, his expression was calm. "I will confess I read the newspaper accounts of your husband's case," he said. "As you mentioned, I shared an interest with him. The collecting community is, after all, not that large. It's possible he and I attended some of the same lectures or seminars over the years, but I have no recollection of it."

"Of course." His answer disappointed her. Perhaps she'd clung to the hope that, if Father Connelly had known Derek, he'd rush to her late husband's defense and somehow convince her that Derek was as innocent as Ariana thought. The idea that he could have been guilty of a crime—and that she had been completely oblivious to that side of him—still stung. What else had she not known about her husband? Or about Ariana even? Was it possible Ariana had, as so many suggested, met someone and run away without bothering to tell even her mother?

"Was there anything else I can help you with?" Father Connelly asked, pulling her from her fog of reverie.

"No, thank you." She shook her head. "I should go now." Though she could find no overt reason to dislike the priest, talking with him made her uncomfortable.

She left the library and told herself from now on she would avoid the room. It held too many reminders of her husband and her daughter and, while she'd gone there initially hoping for comfort, she had found only more mysteries, as enigmatic and unanswerable as the impassive faces of the Greek statues in the display case.

KATHERINE TIED HER SCARF more firmly around her head and looked out over the tops of villas to the turquoise-and-white waves of the Mediterranean visible from the convertible Charles had rented in Monte Carlo. "I don't remember so many houses before," she said.

"It's been nineteen years. I imagine a lot has changed."

She supposed it would have been too much to hope that things would stay the same in this paradise where her marriage had begun so many years ago. She had re-membered it as a land of fast cars, dazzling sun, beautiful people and endless vistas.

Charles downshifted and slowed as the traffic be-came more congested on the outskirts of Monte Carlo. "There's definitely more traffic now," he grumbled.

She laughed. "I remember how you frightened me back then, racing along the coast road as if you were a Grand Prix racer."

He glanced at her. "You were frightened? You never said anything."

"You didn't notice my white face and the way I

braced myself against the dashboard and sucked in my breath at every turn?"

He shook his head. "I thought you were in awe of the scenery."

Through the space between two tall new buildings—hotels, she thought—she could just make out a thin slice of beach. "Yes, I was in awe of the scenery. I was in awe of everything." She glanced back at him. "I was in awe of you." She'd been so in love then, amazed that she was the wife of such a handsome, smart man. Charles was the perfect man for her and she was sure their marriage would be a legendary love to rival that of Grace Kelly and Prince Rainier.

But even legendary loves had to try to survive in a real world of raising children, tending to businesses and coping with loss. She and Charles had been through a lot—they'd raised a beautiful daughter and both had started successful businesses. They'd struggled with the disappointment of not being able to have more children and survived the death of her mother and his father.

All those events took a toll on romance. Maybe she was being foolish to want to relive that heady feeling of first love. Maybe those emotions were only for the young, who didn't know any better.

They drove as far as Beaulieu, but the overlook she remembered from her honeymoon was now blocked by condos. Disappointed, they turned the car around. "Let's head back to Monte Carlo for lunch," Charles said. "Do you remember the name of the café there we liked so much?"

"Belles-amies," she said. "I doubt it's still there."

But it was there. The relief she felt upon seeing it was disproportionate to the occasion. There were no doubt many other places in the tiny principality of Monaco where they could have enjoyed a pleasant lunch. But the fact that this one remnant of her honeymoon trip still remained lifted some of the gloom that had been building on their drive up the now-unfamiliar coast.

They sat on the terrace and ordered mussels in wine, French bread, fresh asparagus in herbs and a crisp chardonnay. The breeze brought the scent of the ocean, overlaid with a hint of expensive perfume from a nearby diner who carried herself with the élan of someone very wealthy, very famous, or both.

"Who do you think she is?" Katherine asked, leaning close to whisper to Charles as they watched a waiter light a cigarette for the woman.

He shrugged. "An actress or model? Or maybe the trophy wife of some rich old man."

"Do you ever think of trading me in for some trophy wife?" The question was out before she could suppress it.

He looked up from his mussels, his expression puzzled. "Why would you ask a question like that?"

She shrugged. "It happens. Remember Henry Adamson from Pershing Limited?" Charles's firm had done a great deal of business with Pershing at one time. "He married that young woman. She couldn't have been more than twenty-two. And that man from your office— Elliot? His second wife was very young, as well."

"I believe that was his third wife." Charles frowned. "And, no, I have no intention of trading you in. Certainly not for some girl with whom I'm sure I'd have nothing in common."

She toyed with her asparagus, then took a long drink of wine. In for a penny, in for a pound... "Sadie Bennett told me she was sure her husband, Derek, was cheating on her. She said he traveled so much for his job, so it was easy for him to meet women and to hide them from her."

"Is that what's got you thinking this way?" Charles's mood lifted. "You don't have to worry about me."

She studied him, trying to read his feelings in his eyes. At one time she was certain she knew him so well; now she realized how difficult it was to tell what a normally unemotional man was thinking. "So you've never been tempted by the women you meet in your travels?"

"I didn't say I'd never been tempted, only that I'd never given in to temptation." His eyes met hers, his normally placid expression replaced by a look of great intensity. "I've never met a woman who interested me as much as you."

His words stirred her, and she laid aside her fork, unable to eat another bite. Maybe she had been a little unfair to Charles. So what if he was not an emotional man? He was a strong one, who felt things deeply, even if he didn't show them. He had wept at her mother's funeral, moved by Alexandra's passing. And he had never failed to be there when Katherine really needed him.

They left the restaurant and strolled, hand in hand, through the streets of old Monaco-ville. They passed the Grand Casino, with its wedding-cake facade and manicured gardens. "Do you want to go in?" Charles asked.

She glanced at him. "Do you?" When they were here on their honeymoon, they'd played blackjack in the American room. Charles had won two thousand francs and used the proceeds to buy her a Hermès scarf, which she still owned, but seldom wore.

He shook his head. "I'm sure I used up all my beginner's luck when we were here before."

She smiled, pleased that he'd been thinking of that long-ago day, as well. A new lover might make new memories with you, but there was much to be said for savoring the ones you shared with a longtime love.

As they stood waiting for the light to change, Tom Diamantopoulos emerged from the casino. He saw them and waved. Or rather, he waved at Katherine, his smile all for her.

Beside her, Charles stiffened.

When they had crossed the street and boarded the elevator to take them down to a lower street, Charles said, "I believe Tom has a crush on you."

If she had not been holding firmly to the railing, she might have stumbled, the remark startled her so. "What makes you think that?" she asked.

"The way he looks at you." He glanced at her again, his expression unreadable. "Men know these things."

How did men know these things? She was familiar with women's intuition, but did men have their own kind of awareness?

"I had no idea."

"I don't blame him." He waited for her to exit the elevator ahead of him. "You're an attractive woman."

Was this a subtle warning that he was aware of her attraction to Tom? Was he letting her know he was watching her, or was she allowing her own sense of guilt to plant ideas in her head?

They walked along the Avenue Saint-Martin, toward the Monaco Cathedral and Princess Grace's tomb. Katherine remembered the mourners who had gathered at the tomb when she and Charles had visited before, only five years after the princess's death. She had been touched by the floral tributes to the American actress who had become royalty.

"Isn't that your father and Sadie?"

Katherine looked in the direction Charles indicated and saw her father's familiar figure arm in arm with the petite American widow. The shock of seeing them together was not so new now; she could even admit some happiness that her father was so clearly enjoying himself, though she could not let go entirely of her worries about the relationship.

"I want him to be happy," she said out loud. "I guess I hadn't thought much about how lonely he must have been since Mother died."

Charles squeezed her hand. "You and your father are a lot alike," he said. "I'm sure he'll be careful."

"I hope so." She glanced up at him, enjoying the feel of his arm so securely around her. "They say love can blind people to danger."

"They say a lot of things that may or may not be true."

And who was to say familiarity didn't blind people to the love that was right under their noses? If only she could be sure the distance she felt from Charles was only due to neglect and not some more serious malady that couldn't be cured.

"Are you about ready to go back to the ship?" he asked.

She nodded. "Yes. We have time to rest before dinner." She might even have suggested a little afternoon lovemaking, but the memory of the last time—when her fantasies of Tom had intruded—still unnerved her.

They took the elevator down to their car and turned it in to the rental agency, then boarded the tender to take them out to the ship. Katherine was all smiles as they made their way toward their penthouse, encouraged by how well the day's outing had gone. It was the most time they'd spent in one another's company in months and she felt it had been a good first step in getting to know each other again.

Buoyed by such optimism, the sight of a young woman in tears was especially jarring. Katherine stopped beside her. "What's wrong?" she asked, alarmed.

The woman dabbed at her eyes with a tissue. "It's just awful," she said. "So incredibly sad."

"What is it?" Charles asked.

"You haven't heard?" The woman stared at them, then shook her head. "It's June Westcott—the older woman. The one who's always involved in everything."

Katherine fought to catch her breath. She grabbed the young woman's arm. "What about June? Has she taken ill?"

The woman shook her head. "Not ill." She choked back a fresh sob. "I just found out. They say she's dead."

CHAPTER TWELVE

"JUNE IS DEAD?" Katherine could not make sense of the words.

The woman nodded. "Her husband found her in bed this morning. She must have died in her sleep." She sniffed. "I feel so awful for him."

"Thank you for telling us," Charles said. He gently took Katherine's hands and led her away.

"We should go see Albert," Katherine said. "Make sure he's all right." Though how could he possibly be all right, when the woman he'd loved for more than sixty years was gone?

They found Albert in his quarters near theirs, surrounded by some of the many friends he and June had made among the ship's passengers and crew. One of the stewards was manning the door and showed Katherine and Charles into the living room.

Albert looked up at him, his eyes watery. He had aged ten years in the last twenty-four hours, looking small and stooped as he sat in an upholstered chair, a photo of a smiling June on the table beside him. "We came as soon as we heard," Katherine said. She knelt on the floor beside his chair and took his hand in hers.

"We were so sorry to hear of June's passing," Charles said. "It must have been a great shock."

Albert nodded, turning to look at June's picture. "She had been living on borrowed time for quite a while now," he said. "We didn't tell anyone because we didn't want them to worry, but the doctors told us months ago her heart was bad and that there wasn't really anything they could do. June decided she wanted to pack as much life as possible into whatever time she had left." He smiled. "I think she enjoyed herself more in these last few months than she ever had."

"Then, those episodes where she claimed to have overdone it?" Katherine asked, "that was her heart?"

Albert nodded. "They worried me, but she didn't want to be fussed over. And it was easier to pretend she had plenty of time left. If anyone could live on sheer force of will alone, it was June."

"I still can't believe it." Katherine choked back tears and patted Albert's hand. Being with him now was comforting, remembering how happy he and June had been together.

"Is there anything we can do?" Charles asked. "Do you need help notifying anyone back home, or making arrangements?"

"Thank you, but that's already been taken care of." Albert looked at Katherine. "The captain visited me as soon as he heard, and your father was here, too, Mrs. Stamos, right before you arrived. They've both been immensely helpful."

"What will you do?" Katherine asked.

"I'll be leaving the ship tomorrow at St. Tropez, with

June's body, and we'll fly home to Bath. Our children will meet us and help with the arrangements on that end."

"If there's anything at all we can do to help, you know you only have to ask," Katherine said. "June was such a special person to everyone who met her, and I feel she was my special friend." She swallowed and fought back the tears that threatened to overflow. So many memories—both of June and of helping with the funeral arrangements for her own mother and coping with that grief—welled up inside her.

"There is one thing you can do," Albert said.

She nodded, fighting to remain composed. "Anything."

"The arrangements you made for our vows renewal…"

"Don't worry about them. I'll take care of canceling everything." Canceling those plans would be a great sorrow, but a necessary one.

"Don't cancel them," Albert said. "Rather, there obviously won't be a vows renewal now, but since the arrangements are made, I thought people might use that as a time for remembering June." He glanced at the others gathered in the room. "Some people have mentioned they'd like to have a little memorial ceremony."

"That's a wonderful idea." She squeezed his hand. "June made such an impact on so many people in the short time she was here. I know everyone will want to come."

He nodded, and that ghost of a smile came to his lips once more. "June always did love parties. She'd enjoy being the guest of honor, even in spirit."

"We should let you rest now." Charles patted Albert's shoulder and sent Katherine a pointed look.

She could see now that the poor man was drooping. Possibly the ship's physician had given him something to help him stay calm. In any case, she knew from experience how exhausting grief could be. She rose. "We'll leave you now, but we'll talk again in the morning, before you disembark." She squeezed his hand. "You were so lucky to have had such a perfect marriage for so many years."

His gaze became more focused, intent on her. "There's no such thing as a perfect marriage. Ours certainly wasn't."

The sharpness of his tone surprised her. "But you seemed so happy…"

"Yes, we were happy. And I loved her more the day she died than the day we wed. But no couple stays together sixty years without their share of problems, and we had ours."

"I…I never would have guessed." She shook her head. "You two seemed so…in sync. Truly perfect."

"Call it long years of practice." He patted her hand. "It's easy enough to let the day-to-day grind of work and raising children get in the way of a relationship. There were a few years there when we were both so busy I sometimes looked across the breakfast table and wondered who this stranger was I'd married. But we made up our minds not to stay strangers."

"What did you do?" she asked.

"We worked at getting to know each other. We made time to talk. We went out on dates." He laughed, a short, barking sound. "You don't think these modern-day television counselors invented all that stuff, do you? The truth is, good marriages take the same kind of nurturing that raising children or keeping friends or any other relationship takes. People think all you need is love, when what you really need is mutual respect and the willingness to work together." He sighed. "Though without love, I suppose you don't have that, either. And I did love her." His voice broke. "And I'm going to miss her."

Katherine nodded, tears running unchecked down her cheeks. "I'm so sorry," she whispered, then turned to go.

In the hallway, she turned to Charles. He held her while she wept, for her friend June and for Albert, who seemed so fragile now. Charles patted her back and gave her a handkerchief and said nothing, but his silence and strength were more comforting than any words might have been.

At last, she composed herself enough to walk with him to their rooms. "I never would have guessed that two people who seemed so perfect for each other would have ever had problems."

"There are no perfect people, so I guess it's no surprise there are no perfect marriages."

She nodded, and went into the bathroom to wash her face and comb her hair. Maybe a better word than *perfect* for the kind of marriage she'd thought June and Albert had was *easy*. As in progressing so smoothly and beautifully. The kind of marriage her parents had had.

She could see now how foolish that assessment had

been. Of course her parents' relationship had seemed *easy* to her, their daughter. What parent showed the troubled side of marriage to their child if it could be avoided? It could be her parents had argued and sniped at one another behind closed doors, or had spent long weeks scarcely speaking and she, caught up in her own world, had never noticed.

And, yet, she was convinced they had been mostly happy, as had June and Albert.

Albert's final words had filled her with a hope that transcended her grief. She'd feared her marriage was over because the closeness she'd craved with Charles seemed to have vanished. But maybe all she needed was to find a way to nurture the love she was sure still existed between them. If her marriage wasn't all she wanted it to be right now, then perhaps it was possible to build the marriage she wanted—to work for what she wanted, the way she worked toward a goal in her business.

It wasn't as romantic as the stories she read in books or saw on the movie screen, and it certainly wasn't easy, but thirty years from now she would be able to think back and say the effort was definitely worthwhile.

THE NEXT MORNING, Sadie sat with Elias in the crowded Court of Dreams, where chairs had been set up for June's memorial service. The opulent room was decorated for a wedding, but the mood was solemn. Captain Nikolas Pappas, in his crisp white dress uniform, stood behind a podium at the bottom of the sweeping staircase.

"We are gathered here this day to celebrate the life of June Wescott," Captain Pappas began. "Though most of us knew her only a short time, she made a great impression on us all, as evidenced by our presence here." He glanced at the notes in front of him and continued. "June's husband, Albert, asked that this service not be one of mourning, but of celebration. To that end, I'd like to open with a time for us to share our memories of June. Would anyone like to begin?"

A dancer from the entertainment staff raised her hand, then stood and looked around at the crowd filling the room. "One thing I loved about June was how she treated everyone as a friend. It didn't matter if you were a cabin steward or a hairdresser, or like me, a dancer. Everyone was her friend. One of my best memories is from just a couple of nights ago, when she taught a group of us how to jitterbug. I couldn't believe a woman her age could move like that!"

Laughter rippled through the gathering. The dancer smiled. "She was so much fun. I'm so glad I met her, though I wish I'd had the chance to know her better."

"I remember the lifeboat drill our first day at sea." A male passenger stood and spoke. "June modeled the life vest and had us all in stitches with her antics. I knew right then she was a special lady."

Another passenger recalled June and Albert as winners of the Not-So-Newlywed game, while others shared laughter over her stint as part of the hypnotist's act.

Katherine stood and cleared her throat. The room fell silent, except for the rustle of bodies shifting in chairs. "June and I became good friends in the short time we knew one another," Katherine said. "She was easy to talk to and a good listener. She shared some of her experiences in life and offered good advice." She paused, staring at the floor, fighting for composure. When she looked up again, her eyes shone. "I'm very glad I had the chance to know her."

Elias squeezed Sadie's hand as Katherine sat. She glanced at him and recognized the pride and concern for his daughter that was reflected in his eyes. "She did a good job, putting this together," Sadie whispered to him. "I know it wasn't easy."

"She has her mother's touch with this kind of thing," he said. "I think June would have been pleased."

"I think so, too," Sadie whispered.

Other passengers shared how June had alternately charmed, comforted and educated them. "She was so full of life, it's hard to believe she's gone," one concluded, and many in the audience nodded.

"Yet, as you can see, her memory lives with us still," Captain Pappas said. "And some part of June will stay with us all for many years to come." He consulted his notes again. "She was a tiny woman, barely five feet tall. She was elderly, a group some would discount as not having a great deal to offer. Yet, June Westcott and her husband, Albert, made such a strong impression on us all in her last few days on earth that I dare say she changed lives. She showed us how to truly live life to the fullest. She had a smile for everyone and an enthusiasm that was contagious.

"This celebration today was originally planned as a renewal of the wedding vows she and Albert made sixty years ago. Instead, we take this time to celebrate June and her life. She is the guest of honor at this party to-day and, though she is not with us physically, I am sure she is with us in spirit. So I would ask that, first, we all observe a moment of silence for June, and for Albert, who, as we speak, is starting the long journey home to England with his beloved."

They bowed their heads, the silence heart-wrenching, broken only by the occasional muffled cough or shuffling of feet. Elias squeezed Sadie's hand and she squeezed back, comforted by the silent com-munication.

"Thank you." At the captain's words, everyone raised their heads. "Now, I propose we all raise a toast in June's honor," he said, "eat something decadent that she would have loved and share this special time with loved ones near you. I'm convinced that's what June would have wanted, and we should honor her wishes."

Sadie and Elias followed the others into the Garden Terrace, where the food and drink originally planned for the vows renewal reception awaited. They accepted flutes of champagne and joined in the communal toast to June's memory. The ship's photographer mingled among them, snapping pictures of the event.

Sadie had scarcely lowered her glass when Elias took her hand and pulled her into an alcove at the side of the room. Here, they were hidden from view by twin potted palms. "What are you doing?" she asked, laugh-ing at this turn of events.

"We've discussed before how you tend to bring out my romantic and sentimental side," he said. His eyes danced with the mischief of a boy—and the desires of a man.

"Yes." Her skin tingled with anticipation. He was up to something, but what?

"I've tried to be discreet, but I'm tired of waiting." He took the glass of champagne from her hand and set it on the floor in the corner, then pulled her toward him. "There's something I've wanted to do practically since we met, and I have to think June would approve."

"Oh?" She smiled up at him, her palms pressed against his chest. "And what is that?"

"This," he said, and lowered his mouth to hers.

Sadie could no more have refused Elias's kiss than she could have stopped breathing. The moment his lips touched hers, she surrendered with the feeling that she had been waiting since the day they'd met for this one moment. There was no fumbling or uncertainty in his touch or her response. They moved in unison, bodies pressed together, lips parted, tongues seeking in a gentle, sensual dance that left her breathless. She slid her hands up to his shoulders and held on, in case her legs gave way from the heady rush of feeling that engulfed her.

She felt lighter than air and young as a girl. She would not have dreamed it was possible to be so happy and so sad at the same time. She was fast falling in love with Elias and, yet, the idea terrified her. So much was unsettled in her life.

"I'm crazy about you," she told him, looking into his eyes, a shiver of delight rushing through her at the desire she found there. A desire that matched her own.

"I think you know how I feel about you," he said,

pulling her closer still. There was no mistaking the hard ridge of his erection pressed against her stomach.

She nodded. "But you have to admit, this isn't the time to be starting a new relationship," she said. "So much in my life is unsettled."

"I think June would have said there's never a wrong or right time," he said. "If we wait for things to be perfect, we'll never take a chance on love."

"Then, we'd better take a chance." She'd never risked much in her life. But playing it safe hadn't gotten her very far. Coming on this cruise had been her first real risk and, though she hadn't yet found Ariana, she still hoped she might. And look how that risk had paid off in other ways.

CHAPTER THIRTEEN

As soon as the reception for June was over, Katherine grabbed Charles's hand and pulled him away from his conversation with the captain. "We have to go now," she whispered in her best sultry tone.

Charles looked at her, puzzled. "Go where?" he asked, as he allowed her to lead him out the door.

"I have a surprise for you." As she'd arranged earlier, a steward waited by the departure ramp with their bags. "Charles, could you carry those, please?" she asked, indicating the two overnight bags she'd packed while Charles was in the shower this morning.

"We're leaving the ship?" he asked. "Where are we going? What's gotten into you?"

Of course Mr. Practical wanted answers. She stopped and faced him, arms crossed over her chest. "This isn't going to work if you don't at least play along," she said. "I promise, it's something you'll like. Now, take the bags. Please?"

He hesitated for a moment, studying her, and opened his mouth as if to ask another question, then apparently thought better of it. He accepted the bags from the steward and followed her down the gangplank where a taxi waited.

"You've been busy," Charles said as he handed their luggage to the driver. "How long have you been planning this little getaway?"

"Oh, not long," she said airily, avoiding his gaze, sure if he looked into her eyes, he'd see how close to panic she had been, afraid she wouldn't be able to pull any of this off. Though she'd been promising her father and herself that she would take more time to work on her marriage, June's death had forced her into action. Losing her friend had made her realize how quickly opportunities could be lost and never regained.

She had stayed up late last night, telling Charles she was putting the finishing touches on June's memorial service, but, in reality, plotting this getaway. The ship had docked in St. Tropez. It would spend the night there, then head to Portofino. They would take a short flight the next day to rejoin the cruise. She hoped the respite would grant them a new perspective and a new commitment to each other.

The taxi took them away from the city, past fields full of laborers harvesting grapes. "It was like this when we were here on our honeymoon," Charles said. "Only, they were planting crops instead of harvesting them."

"Yes." She turned to him. "I wanted to recapture a little of that honeymoon feeling again," she said. "It's hard to do on a ship full of people, where neither of us can really get away from our jobs and responsibilities."

"So you decided to kidnap me and steal away." He looked amused.

"Something like that. Do you mind terribly?"

He shook his head and took her hand. "It's like you to think of something like this. You always were the creative one in our marriage, working hard to make things perfect."

Yes. That's what she wanted for these few days—a perfect interlude to allow love to blossom for them again.

"So where are we going?" he asked, facing forward.

"It's a surprise," she said. A surprise for her, as well, since she'd reserved the place based solely on a blurry picture on a Web site and the fact that it was available on short notice. But it had been in the same area where they'd spent part of their honeymoon, and the leasing agent had assured her it was "beautiful, clean and very romantic."

Romance was exactly what she was looking for—the antidote to the complacency that threatened to destroy their marriage. They were no longer carefree youngsters in the first throes of passion, but they had to regain a little of the fire that had brought them together or risk growing too cold and lifeless to bear. Recreating a little of their honeymoon and learning to relate to each other as lovers again had seemed the perfect answer to her desperate mind.

She only prayed it would work. She refused to go on with the marriage as it had been, living as polite strangers. June had showed her life was an adventure to be filled with emotion, and Tom had awakened her to the fact that she was still a desirable woman who wanted to be defined by more than her role as a mother or as a capable businessperson.

People talked about love at first sight all the time.

She only hoped love could be renewed with a second, closer look at each other.

DANTE WOKE TO DARKNESS, the smell of diesel fuel and fish stinging his nose, rough rope digging into his wrists and ankles. His head pounded and his stomach rolled. He struggled past the sickness and pain, trying to think clearly. He had a dim memory of a struggle with a large man…his mind cleared further and he remembered that he and Ariana had been captured by two thugs who were not Camorra. They had been taken in the small boat to a larger vessel, and Dante had made one last effort to escape, which resulted in him being hit in the head again.

Ariana! He tried to sit up, but it was impossible in the narrow space where he was being held. As his vision adjusted to the darkness, he could see he was in the hold of a ship, surrounded by coils of rope and rusty metal that served as ballast.

Unable to sit, he tried to roll onto his back, and collided with something soft and yielding. "Ariana?" he called. Then louder, "Ariana!"

No answer. He clenched his fist against the fear and rage that engulfed him. If those thugs had harmed Ariana…

He took a deep breath, struggling for calm. He needed all his wits about him. The steady throb of the engine and rhythmic slap of waves against the hull told him they were moving at a moderate rate of speed. He did not know how long he had been unconscious, but reasoned they had been traveling for some time.

Most likely, they were headed somewhere specific. If the thugs had only wanted to hide out, they could have anchored at sea.

The fact that he was still alive was promising. His captors could have easily killed him and dumped his body overboard.

If he was alive, then Ariana was alive, as well. He held on to that hope. The last he had seen of her, she had been lying beside him in the Zodiac. But it was then that he had struggled with his captors, earning him another blow to the head, and oblivion. He hoped Ariana, being more cooperative, had been spared any injury. Perhaps, even now, she was up top, safe, though surely frightened.

He stretched out his fingers, exploring the bonds at his wrists. Thick rope wrapped many times. He looked around at the debris scattered in the small space. He could find something here to use as a weapon and ambush his captors when they came down to retrieve him, as they surely would when they arrived at their destination. If he could take the gun from one of them, it would even the odds considerably.

In the crowded, narrow space any movement at all was difficult. Bound hand and foot, he was reduced to scooting along the floor one painful centimeter at a time.

Footsteps overhead froze him. Light poured into the small space as a hatch was raised, temporarily blinding him. He squinted toward the dark figure who leaned down toward him. "Be still down there!" the man barked.

Dante said nothing. If his captor thought something was wrong, he might come down to investigate. At close quarters, Dante would have more of a chance to overpower him.

"Do not think you can trick me," the man said, as if reading Dante's thoughts. "I know your kind. You are a fighter."

Still, Dante said nothing.

"We are almost at our destination," the man continued. "Then we will take you off the ship. I warn you not to try to fight us, then. If you do, we will make sure the woman suffers for your actions."

Dante's throat tightened at the mention of Ariana. He wanted to ask if she was all right, but would not give this thug the satisfaction of knowing she mattered to him. "Where are you taking us?" he asked.

"Somewhere where you will be out of the way. Unable to cause trouble."

Trouble for whom? Dante wondered. The Camorra, or someone else? And were his captors most concerned about him—or about Ariana?

He forced himself to relax as much as possible against the hard floor. He needed to conserve his energy for whatever lay ahead. When they arrived at whatever their destination would be, his first order of business was to determine, once and for all, what Ariana Bennett was really up to. Was she his ally, or his enemy?

"I will come again for you shortly," the man said. "Remember—if you cooperate, nothing more will happen to the woman."

Nothing *more*. What had they done to her already?

Dante ground his teeth together, frustrated by his help-lessness. The man straightened, and then the hatch lowered again, plunging Dante into a darkness that seemed much blacker than before.

A SHORT DRIVE from St. Tropez was the village of Plan de la Tour, a collection of old stone houses on shady streets set in the midst of vineyards. The taxi stopped in front of a leaning iron gate in a crumbling rock wall. "One twenty-six Rue du Jean," the driver announced.

Katherine stared at the dilapidated wall and swallowed hard. "Are you sure?" She dug in her purse and retrieved the computer printout confirming her reservation. "One twenty-six Rue du Jean," she read, and stared at the same numbers painted on the gate.

"You rented a villa?" Charles asked.

She nodded, and forced a smile. "I'm sure it looks much better inside. The rental agent said it was beautiful and charming."

"I always thought charming was real estate code for needs a lot of work," he said. But he followed her out of the taxi and around to the trunk, where the driver retrieved their luggage and Katherine paid the fare.

Charles led the way through the gate and down a walkway that was missing half its bricks. She retrieved the key from the hiding place the leasing agent had told her about and opened the door, afraid of what she'd find on the other side.

"This isn't so bad," Charles said, setting down their bags just inside the door and walking to the middle of the front room.

"It really isn't, is it?" The apprehension that had gripped her loosened its hold, and she even smiled as she studied the high, white walls and elegant furnishings. The decor was simple and clean and just old-fashioned enough to live up to the agent's billing as romantic.

"It reminds me of the place we stayed on our honeymoon," she said, taking his hand.

"It does, doesn't it?" His smile warmed her. *This is going to work,* she thought, her spirits soaring.

They explored the rest of the house—dining room, kitchen, bathroom and bedroom, complete with a large iron bedstead and what she was sure was a real feather bed.

Charles sat on the side of the bed and pulled her to him. She stood between his legs, hands on his shoulders, his hands at her waist. "This is reminding me more and more of our honeymoon," he said, with a wicked grin. His hands slid to her bottom and pulled her closer still, his lips finding hers, his kiss at once insistent and languid, as if to say that he wanted her now but intended to take his time enjoying her.

She responded with an enthusiasm born of relief as much as desire. She wanted so much for everything about these next two days to be perfect, a symbolic new beginning for their marriage.

After a long while, they drew apart, both flushed and a little breathless. Charles caressed her bottom, sending tingles of awareness up and down her spine, the tension building between her thighs. It had been a long time since her husband had aroused her so and she planned to savor the feeling. She wanted the anticipation of them being together to build all afternoon until, when they did finally come together, the results were truly memorable.

She shifted over to sit in his lap and brushed the hair back from his forehead. "Do you remember the first thing we did when we got to the villa then?" she asked.

He frowned, obviously searching for the correct answer. Then his expression brightened. "We took a bath."

"A bubble bath." She was delighted he remembered. "We were both so hot and sweaty from the long ride here. I remember you washed my hair. I thought it was the most romantic thing anyone had ever done." The sensation of his strong fingers massaging her scalp, the utter relaxation of leaning back in his arms and the caring the gesture represented had made her feel so loved and so desirable. She longed to recapture that feeling.

He grinned. "A bubble bath sounds pretty good about now."

She laughed. "I was hoping you'd say that. I brought bubbles."

They gathered their bath things and headed for the bathroom, with its huge white claw-foot tub and high clerestory windows propped open to the autumn breeze. She laid out everything, then leaned over to turn on the water.

The white porcelain knob turned and turned in her hand, but nothing happened. "There's no water," she said, looking over her shoulder at Charles.

"Here, let me try." He moved past her and turned the

knob. When that didn't work, he cranked it harder. With an awful wrenching sound that made Katherine's teeth ache, the knob broke off in his hand.

"Charles!" She put her hand to her mouth and stared at the knob and the jagged edge of metal where it had once been connected. A single rusty drop clung to the edge of the opening, then landed with a splat in the bottom of the tub.

"That wasn't supposed to happen." He fit the broken edges of pipe and handle together and frowned. Then he walked over to the sink and turned the faucet there. It, too, was dry. "I don't think we have any water in the house."

"What are we going to do?" she asked.

He tossed the handle onto the rug and pulled her close. "I say we forget the bath and go back to the bedroom."

And, after they made love, she'd still want a bath. "How are we going to cook or wash dishes or use the toilet without water?" she asked.

"We could go to a hotel."

Yes, a hotel would be the practical solution. But she was sick to death of being practical and sensible. The whole idea behind this getaway had been to seek out romance. To be alone in a little villa in the country, as they had been on their honeymoon. To recapture some of the spirit of adventure and fun with which they had started their lives together. "Maybe you could fix the plumbing?" she said.

He released her, a frown cutting deep furrows into his forehead. "I'll see what I can do."

Charles was not handy. Not with tools. He didn't

have to be. He knew everything there was to know about architecture and his success in that field allowed him to hire others to be handy for him.

But now she fervently wished he was one of those geniuses at fixing things, the type of husband other women sometimes bragged about.

"We'd better find some tools," he said, leading the way out of the bathroom. Forty-five minutes later, they'd unearthed a hammer, an ancient-looking wrench, a screwdriver, a pry bar and enough spiderwebs to give Katherine nightmares for weeks.

"What do you want me to do?" she asked anxiously as Charles prepared to attack the broken pipes.

"Why don't you see if you can find us something to eat?" he said, not looking up from his attempts to turn the pipe with the wrench.

She hurried away, telling herself she should be more annoyed at being relegated to the kitchen, but grateful she didn't have to stand by and watch Charles swear and sweat over plumbing that was probably beyond hope.

The kitchen was well stocked and she soon laid out an al fresco supper—wine, bread, cheese and olives. A romantic meal that would please the palate and the other senses. She began to feel better about their prospects.

Supper assembled, she checked on Charles. She found him with his sleeves rolled up, sweat pouring down the side of his face, muttering a steady stream of unintelligible curses as he wrestled the recalcitrant pipes. "How are you doing?" she asked brightly.

"This plumbing is decrepit. It must date to World

War II." He wiped his brow with his shirt sleeve. "And even then it probably didn't work properly."

"Maybe we should call a plumber," she said.

"It's Friday afternoon. No one will come."

He was right. A local plumber would laugh at the idea of coming out to help a tourist—provided she could even find one who would answer the phone.

"Let's forget about the plumbing for a while," she said. "I opened a bottle of wine and put together some supper."

"That sounds like an excellent idea." He tossed aside the wrench. She winced as it hit the bottom of the tub with a clang. Then she fixed another smile on her face. They'd both feel better with food and wine. Then maybe they'd retire to that comfortable bed upstairs. There was still a chance to have the perfect second honeymoon. They just had to be flexible.

A good quality for any marriage, she reminded herself.

An especially good one for second honeymoons gone wrong.

CHAPTER FOURTEEN

KATHERINE LED CHARLES to the table where she'd spread their romantic feast. The arrangement of bread, wine and cheese looked like a still life. Or an advertisement for an expensive deli. "I'm starved," Charles said. He reached for the bottle of wine and the two wineglasses. Just as he started to pour, the light over the table flickered and went out.

"What now?" Katherine walked over to the wall and flicked the light switch back and forth. Nothing happened.

"Maybe it's a fuse," Charles said. "I'll check." He disappeared into the kitchen. Katherine winced as she heard doors opening and closing, the clatter of pots and pans and much mysterious shuffling of objects. She frowned at the table, then plucked an olive from the plate and popped it into her mouth. Then she poured a glass of wine and pulled out a chair. She'd sit here and drink…and drink some more. By the time Charles returned she'd either be mellow or drunk, but at least she wouldn't be the nervous wreck she was now.

One glass of wine later, Charles returned. He had cobwebs in his hair and smudges of dirt on one cheek.

"It's not a fuse," he said. "As far as I can tell, the electricity is out for the whole house."

"Probably faulty wiring to go with the bad plumbing." She pulled the wine bottle closer. "Would you like a drink?"

"Pour me a glass and I'll get some candles," he said. "I think I saw some in the kitchen."

He returned shortly with several candles, none of them the same size and all of them in odd colors ranging from orange to a bilious green. Katherine, feeling strangely detached, watched as he lit them and stuck them to saucers. They made an unsightly arrangement in the middle of the table.

"I guess a candlelight dinner isn't so bad," Charles said, sitting next to her.

"Hmm." She drank more wine and stared at the orange and green candles. Not exactly her idea of romantic.

Charles filled his plate, then turned to her. "Aren't you going to eat?"

She shook her head and reached for the bottle. "I'm not very hungry. I think I'll have some more wine."

He gave her a curious look, then turned back to his plate.

She watched him as he ate. He was so calm, so unmoved by anything. When they had first met, she had seen this placidness as a sign of strength. His coolness was an antidote to her own sometimes fevered moods.

Over the years, some of her earlier fire had cooled, but Charles had taken on little of her warmth. Not that he was a cold man. During lovemaking and in certain emotional moments, particularly with Gemma, he could be quite demonstrative.

But, most of the time, his reserved exterior was a shell over whatever truth lay within.

Meal finished, he laid aside his knife and fork and pushed his plate away, then turned to her. "Is something wrong?" he asked.

She finished the wine. "What makes you think something's wrong?"

"You haven't said a word for the last ten minutes and you're practically staring a hole through me."

She took a deep breath and said the words that had crowded the back of her throat for the last few hours. "I think I want a divorce."

The awful words hung in the air, forming an icy curtain between them.

Charles stared at her, heart pounding. "What did you say?" he asked, though her words repeated themselves over and over in his brain. *Divorce. Divorce. Divorce…*

"I…" She turned her head away. "We don't have a marriage anymore, Charles. We're just two people living in the same house. Polite strangers."

"Is that how you see me? As a stranger?" How could she say that, when he felt as if he knew her better than he knew himself? He knew every inch of her body, every part of her history. But, as he studied her now, searching her face for some clue as to her real feelings, he realized with a sinking feeling that she was right; he didn't know her now. This woman who wanted to end the marriage he had been so sure of was a stranger to him.

"We've grown apart," she said. "It happens sometimes. I'd hoped this trip would help us grow close again, but it isn't happening." She shrugged, as if this was sufficient explanation for her shocking announcement.

"Is there someone else?" he asked. He thought of Tom Diamantopoulos. The chief engineer was young and handsome and obviously infatuated with Katherine. Did she return his feelings?

Her eyes widened and she looked stunned. "No!" She shook her head. "No, there isn't anyone else."

The first shock was receding, replaced by the anger of a wounded animal. "You planned this getaway to tell me you want to end our marriage?" he asked after a moment, his voice strained.

She shook her head. "No... I... I don't know." She bowed her head, hands knotted in her lap.

He stared at her, saying nothing. He wanted to plead with her, to demand she take the words back, but his lips remained welded shut, his brain too numb to come up with any coherent speech. The only sound was of a fly buzzing on a nearby windowsill and the occasional sputtering of one of the candles.

"Is this really what you want?" When he finally spoke, his voice was thin, as he struggled to squeeze the words out.

She buried her face in her hands. "I don't know. I only know I can't go on like this."

He looked at the floor. "I see. And you've made this decision without consulting me."

"This isn't like picking out the design for a new building or deciding which car to buy," she snapped.

"What is there to consult about? You're always working and, even when you're home, we can't have a conversation about anything but Gemma or where to eat dinner."

Her words stung him, and he took a step back. "And that's all my fault?"

"Well, it's not mine. I've been trying for months to reach you and…and you just aren't there for me anymore."

He glared at her, eyes burning, fists knotted at his side. What did she want from him? Did she want a partner who followed after her like a besotted schoolboy? Or someone who had no interests outside of her? He'd done everything he could to support her, to encourage her independence and her dreams. He'd worked hard to make sure marrying him did not mean giving up any of the material comforts with which she'd been raised. Did all that mean nothing to her?

"Don't just stand there!" she demanded, the harshness of her voice shattering the silence between them. "Convince me we shouldn't do this."

"What do you want me to say? You seem to have your mind made up." If he had thought begging would make any difference, he would have been tempted to fall on his knees before her, but, if she had already made up her mind to leave him, he was determined to at least keep his pride intact.

They glared at each other, no warmth in their expressions. The few feet between them might have been a chasm; they could find no bridge to cross it. Charles clenched his fists until his nails bit into his flesh; he welcomed the pain. Anything to distract him from the tearing in his heart. The woman he had loved almost half his life had as much as admitted she no longer loved him. He didn't know how to fight that reality, so he stood frozen, trapped by pride and pain and the fear that, if he took even a single step toward her, he would break down altogether.

Katherine waited for Charles to speak, his silence more damning than any words. Apparently, he didn't think she was worth fighting for. He stood there, not looking at her, but through her. She could feel his anger, even across the room. As if all of this was her fault alone. As if the only thing wrong with their marriage was that she wouldn't accept it as it was.

She couldn't stay in the room with him one minute longer. She stood, knocking over her chair in her haste, and raced down the hall and up the narrow flight of stairs to the bedroom.

Once there, she pulled one of the pillows and half the blankets from the bed and ran to the door with them. "You can sleep on the sofa!" she called, and hurled the bedding down the stairs.

Then she shut the door and locked it and fell on the bed, painful sobs ripped from her throat. *So this is how it ends,* she thought.

She had expected to feel more relief. To experience a lessening of the awful tension that had gripped her for weeks. But she felt only intense pain, as if someone had wrenched a vital organ from her body.

Oh, God, what a fool she'd been! She wept into the

one remaining pillow until it was soaked. She could have filled that claw-foot tub with her tears, she thought ruefully, but without Charles to bathe there with her, what did it matter?

AFTER JUNE'S memorial service, Elias asked Sadie to have lunch with him in St. Tropez the next day. "There's someone I want you to meet," he said.

She waited for him to elaborate further, but he said nothing more. She agreed to accompany him, her curiosity growing. In her previous interactions with him, Elias had been concerned, confident, courtly, even playful. She had never seen him as preoccupied as he was right now.

His uneasiness continued the next day when they met for their lunch date. She had to repeat her question about local wineries twice in the taxi on the way to the restaurant and, when he finally acknowledged her, his answer was short to the point of brusqueness. He continually drummed his fingers against the armrest in the backseat of the taxi and checked his watch at least twice in the ten-minute drive to the restaurant. She might have believed a different man to be nervous, but what would Elias have to be nervous about?

When they entered the restaurant, a younger man came forward to greet them. Tall and tanned, with dark curly hair touched at the temples with gray, he had the muscular build and rugged complexion of an outdoorsman. Sadie watched as the two men shook hands. The younger man seemed so familiar to her, yet, she was sure she'd never met him before.

Elias put his hand on her arm. "Sadie, I'd like you to meet Theo Catomeris, my son."

He continued the introduction, but Sadie was suddenly deaf to his words. Elias had only mentioned his two daughters to her before now. And she didn't miss Theo's different last name. She turned to Elias, her eyes full of questions, but he slid his gaze away from her, back to Theo.

"Its so nice to meet you, Mrs. Bennett." Theo took her hand and bent low. Sadie bit back a smile. The son was every bit as charming as the father, it seemed. She wondered if Katherine and her sister knew about this young man? Had Alexandra?

They made small talk as they studied the menu— innocuous comments on the weather and traffic. Sadie wondered again why Elias had brought her. Was Elias introducing her to Theo as a sign of how serious he was about her? The thought sent a shiver through her—not of apprehension, but of pleasure.

But, as she continued to watch the two men together, she realized another possibility—maybe Elias had invited her along because he wasn't entirely at ease in Theo's presence. Outwardly, he appeared as confident as ever, but there were little signs of his discomfort—his unaccustomed garrulousness and the close way he studied Theo's every move. She had the feeling she was watching two people who were still getting to know each other. Could it be that Theo had only recently come into his father's life?

"You've been sending a lot of business my way," Theo said after they had ordered.

"Your tours are very popular with passengers on *Alexandra's Dream.*" Elias turned to Sadie. "Theo operates a tour company that offers sailing tours between Corfu and Kefalonia. He's been very successful." She didn't miss the note of pride in Elias's voice.

"I have an exclusive contract to provide tours to Argosy Cruises," Theo said. "Something Elias insisted on." He sat back, a teasing smile on his lips. "He paid handsomely for the privilege."

Their food arrived and, for a time, they devoted their full attention to the peppered beef and the lamb with rosemary and garlic. "You made a good choice for the restaurant," Elias complimented Theo. He looked around the airy dining room with its abundance of greenery and glass. "I'll suggest we add it to our list of recommended places for our passengers."

"The chef is a friend," Theo said. "He has a commitment to using local produce and meats and supporting organic farmers."

Elias laughed. "Of course." To Sadie he explained. "Theo is passionate about ecology and wildlife. He's established a fund to protect the wild horses of Ainos and other wildlife on the island of Kefalonia."

"That's very admirable," she said.

"He's even inspired me to use more of my resources for the betterment of the environment," Elias said.

Theo nodded. "He's learning."

The atmosphere at the table grew less tense. "How are you liking Florida?" Elias asked.

"It's very different from Europe, but I'm enjoying it," Theo said. "I return to Corfu once a month or so to take care of my business."

"And Trish? I trust she's well?"

Theo's smile broadened. "Trish is wonderful."

"Good. It's good to see you happy."

Sadie didn't have any idea who Trish was but decided to ask Elias later.

Theo inquired after Katherine and Helena. "I'm sure it was a great shock to them to learn I existed," he said to Sadie. "But they've been nothing but gracious." He smiled, a look so like Elias's own that Sadie felt her heart stutter in its rhythm. "After so many years of being an only child, it's been nice knowing I have other family out there," he added.

"They were happy to welcome you," Elias said. He did not add that he was happy, also, though Sadie sensed that he was. Why was it so difficult for men to say such things to each other?

"My mother says hello," Theo said.

Elias frowned but said nothing—which in itself spoke volumes to Sadie. Whatever his relationship with Theo's mother had once been, Elias now apparently held her in contempt, though he was too great a gentleman to say as much to her son.

They parted with thanks for the pleasant afternoon and promises to stay in touch. "Let's walk," Elias said. "I'm not ready to go back to the ship yet. We should see some of St. Tropez while we have the chance."

"Theo seems like a very pleasant man," she said, walking with him past shops and restaurants.

"His grandparents can take credit for that," Elias said. "I had nothing to do with raising him, and his mother had little to do with him, as well."

"Is it his mother you don't like, or the idea that you once chose her as your lover?"

Elias stopped and looked at her, his expression grim. At first, she feared she'd angered him. Then his countenance relaxed. "You're very perceptive," he said. "I imagine it's both. I was young and foolish and she was beautiful and clever."

He let out a heavy breath. "I soon learned that Anastasia Catomeris is completely without conscience. As soon as she learned of my family's wealth, she became determined to have me. She swore she was taking birth control pills, then mysteriously became pregnant."

"Women do occasionally become pregnant while on the pill," Sadie said.

"Not Anastasia. She knew exactly what she was doing when she became pregnant. She expected I would marry her and she would have me and my family's fortune. I was not so blinded by lust that I didn't realize which of those two she valued most. When I told her I wouldn't marry her, she flew into a rage."

"I can see why you wouldn't want to marry someone like that." It was the least judgmental thing she could think of to say. This picture of Elias as a young, privileged playboy being taken in by a beautiful seductress was a new one for her; it showed a side of him that was not as attractive as the image she had formed of him as the grieving widower, devoted father and successful businessman. Perhaps a more realistic side. In a way, it was comforting to know that someone as seemingly perfect as Elias had flaws. Flaws he was not afraid to expose to her.

The idea warmed her, and she reached out and squeezed his hand.

He returned the gesture and they started walking again. They turned onto the Quai Jean Jaures and looked out over the deep blue waters of the Bay of Saint-Tropez and the lines of yachts snugged against the docks. Sadie thought how fitting it was that she was here, in one of the most romantic cities in the world, with a man who had made her believe in romance once again.

"I know I wasn't entirely blameless in the matter," Elias said after a moment. "And it still pains me to think how many years I wanted nothing to do with my son. I sent money to support him but otherwise pretended he didn't exist." He glanced at her. "I told myself I needed to spare Alexandra and my daughters that shame, but I can admit now, I was sparing myself. I hated that anyone would know how foolish I'd been."

She tucked her hand in the crook of his arm and squeezed. "Did Alexandra ever find out about Theo?" she asked.

"Not for many years." He shoved his hands in his pockets and his shoulders slumped. "She was hurt at first when I told her, but she was a very sensible woman. She believed me when I said my involvement with Tasia was over before we met. When she'd recovered from her initial shock, she urged me to acknowledge Theo, to get to know him as a father should know his son." He shook his head. "I refused to even consider the idea. It upset her a great deal."

She heard the regret in his voice, but could think of no words of comfort.

He glanced at her. "It was one of the few serious disagreements we'd ever had."

"What prompted you to change your mind—to finally get to know him?" she asked.

The lines etched across his forehead and around his mouth deepened. "Business. Soon after I purchased the Liberty Line, I learned that one of our most popular tour providers had refused to renew their contract with us. Liberty was a new project for me," he continued. "One I was determined would succeed. I didn't know Theo owned the tour company, but I felt the refusal to contract with us was an insult."

Sadie nodded. Elias was not a man who would easily suffer a blow to his pride. "Did Theo know you owned the cruise line? And that you were his father?"

"Yes. When I discovered that, his refusal became a personal insult."

"What did you do?"

Elias's expression darkened. "I'm not particularly proud of my actions now. I first attempted to bully him into continuing to do business with my company. Then I tried to bribe him."

"Elias!" she chided. "How could you think a son of yours would respond to either tactic?"

A faint smile eased Elias's severe expression. "I didn't know him as well then."

"Obviously, the two of you were finally able to come to some agreement," she said.

He nodded. "By this time, he had met his sisters and they both went to work on me, as well as the young woman whose company brokered the various shore excursions and extra tours for us." His smile expanded. "That woman, Trish Melrose, and Theo are now living together in Florida for much of the year, where her business is based."

"So he should feel kindly toward you for bringing them together, if nothing else."

He took her hand in his and squeezed it. "I respect him for standing up for his principles. As you said, he is my son."

"It's a wise man who can admit he was wrong," Sadie said. "And now you and your son can build a relationship as men."

He nodded. "For years, I put him out of my mind. It was as if he didn't exist. I believed my daughters were enough. They were everything a man could want in children. But, when I met Theo—when he became flesh and blood to me and not just an abstract idea…" He cleared his throat. "To look at him and know I had a son was the most incredible feeling. Entirely unexpected. I have no right to be proud of him, but I respect and admire the way he conducts himself and the success he's made of his business. And the person he is."

His voice held more emotion than she could remember hearing.

"It's good you haven't let your feelings for his mother sour your relationship with your son," she said.

He nodded. "If anything, the experience with her taught me to be more cautious with women. I'm sure that's part of the reason I've been so hesitant to start a new relationship after Alexandra died."

"There's no time limit on mourning a loved one's passing," she said. "There are some who would say I haven't mourned my husband enough." She raised her head. "But I refuse to feel guilty about that. I'd be a fool to let the chance to love a good man pass me by."

He squeezed her hand. "And it may be I was waiting for the right woman to come along before I let go of my grief and my caution."

Caution. Something common sense and previous experience told her she should exercise with Elias. After all, she'd known the man only a few days. But, when he looked into her eyes, it was as if he looked into her heart and saw the woman inside her who had been waiting so long for love.

CHAPTER FIFTEEN

WHEN KATHERINE EMERGED from the bedroom the next morning, she crept down the stairs weighted down with dread. What could she say to the man she had loved for so long? To the father of her child? Were there any words that would get them through the awful settling of property and severing of what they had built together? Of what they had so inexplicably lost?

But the kitchen was empty, as was the dining room, where the remains of last night's supper mocked her. Her romantic picnic meal was no longer fit for anything but the garbage. Her stomach roiled at the site of the empty wine bottle and the stale bread, and her head throbbed from the effects of too much wine and too many tears.

She sat in a chair against the dining room wall, pulling the cardigan she wore tight around her. Had Charles left her here to find her own way back to the ship? Was he even now making arrangements to fly home, as far from her as he could get?

The back door opened and she turned toward the sound, heart in her throat. Charles appeared in the doorway of the room where she sat. His hair was uncombed and he still wore the wrinkled clothes he'd had on last night. "I thought you'd left," she said softly.

He ran his hand over his chin, beard stubble making a rasping sound in the dead silence of the house. "I went for a walk," he said. "We need to talk."

How ironic that after all the months of silence regarding anything significant, now they would have to talk.

But there was so much to decide—questions of support and property and what to tell Gemma.

At the thought of her daughter, fresh tears welled in Katherine's eyes. Would Gemma hate her for doing this? Would she ever understand the desperation that had driven her to even consider such a step? Gemma's sorrow would only add to Katherine's own.

She took a deep breath, determined to remain calm. Reasonable. Charles would be as practical in these manners as in any other. "Sit down," she said.

But he didn't sit. He paced, his hands in his pockets, filling the room with his agitation. "I know we haven't been as close as we could be these last months," he began. "We've both been busy. I never worried. I told myself marriages have cycles like this. That, when things slowed down, we would be all right again."

"I told myself that, too, for a while," she said. She leaned forward, elbows on her knees, and shredded the damp tissue she'd crumpled in her hand. "But we've been alone on a cruise ship more than a week and we still haven't said one really significant thing to each other."

"This is significant," he said, stopping in front of her. "How much more significant could we get?"

She nodded. "I don't want to make this a litany of

who's right and who's wrong. I'm sure we're both at fault. Let's just…" She stared at the red-and-black floral pattern of the sofa, the design blurring before her. "Let's just try to get through this."

"No."

The force of his declaration startled her. She looked up at him, expecting to see fresh anger.

Instead, he dropped to his knees before her and took her hand in his. "I won't 'get through' this," he said. "Tell me what's wrong and I'll do whatever I can to make it better." His voice was gentler than she had heard it in years, rough with tears.

That kindness started her weeping again. She sniffed and wiped at her eyes, struggling to contain her emotions. How could she tell him what was wrong if she was crying a river of tears?

He handed her a handkerchief. The sight of it, neatly pressed and folded, his initials in gold embroidered in one corner, set up a fresh flow of tears. Even the man's handkerchief was precise and orderly!

She blew her nose loudly and wiped her eyes again, smearing black mascara across the crisp white linen, a sight which gave her an absurd amount of satisfaction.

"Charles, do you love me?" she asked.

He looked startled. "Of course I do. You're my wife."

Not exactly the passionate declarations he would have wished for. "My being your wife doesn't mean you love me. It only means you loved me, or at least liked me, enough at one time to marry me."

He leaned forward and took her hand, his expression troubled. "I'm sorry you didn't know the answer to that question. But, yes, I do love you. Very much." He swallowed. "Is the problem that you no longer love me?"

"No. I mean, yes, I love you. But it all feels so one-sided." She pulled her hand from his and laced her fingers together. "Why don't we act like lovers anymore? There are times when I feel more like your secretary, or worse, your mother, than your lover."

"I certainly don't think of you as my mother or my secretary," he said.

"Then, do you even think of me?" She glared at him. "When you're traveling on business, or even when you're at home? Are you really thinking of me, or is your mind on work or on something else entirely?"

"Sometimes it's on all those things." He leaned toward her, elbows on his knees. "I don't understand what you're getting at here."

And that, too, was part of the problem, she wanted to shout. He didn't understand. But she ground her teeth together and held back her rage, determined not to derail this nascent attempt at communication by playing the role of overemotional shrew. "Do you remember when we first married?" she asked, instead, her voice even. "How much time we spent together—taking walks, making love—even just *talking?*"

A deep *V* formed over the bridge of his nose. "We were newlyweds. We didn't have anything else to distract us."

"But, lately, *everything* distracts us," she said. "Our jobs. Social obligations. Even Gemma. When was the last time we spent even four hours at a time with each other? Or had a real conversation?"

"I thought that's what this trip was for."

"Yes, and I had such hopes..." She looked away again, a great weariness dragging at her. "I wanted everything to be perfect between us again, but all I've learned is that we don't know how to be together anymore."

"I don't think you've given us enough of a chance," he said.

She shook her head. "I look at you and I see the man I fell in love with, but I also see a stranger. Someone I don't know at all. Someone whose thoughts I don't know. Whose dreams I have no inkling of."

He sat, head down, for a long moment. She swallowed past the tightness in her throat as she waited for his answer. At that moment, she felt more distanced from him than she ever had.

"I'll admit I never thought much about needing to know those things in a relationship," he said after a while. "It was enough for me, knowing you were there. That you had always been there, part of my life."

"It's not enough for me," she whispered. "I need more." She swallowed hard. "A marriage ought to be more than just being there."

"I see that now." He raised his head and, when his eyes met hers, she was struck by the depth of sadness there. "You know I'm a practical man, not an emotional one. But I don't want to lose you. If that means I have to talk more and do more and be with you more, I'll do it."

He took her hand and held it, so tightly her fingers hurt, but she didn't dare move away. She had waited so long to hear him say these things. "Don't leave without giving me another chance," he said. "Even if I didn't say it enough, I do love you."

"I love you, too," she whispered, her vision blurring with fresh tears. It was true, in spite of the pain surrounding her love. "You don't think things have gone too wrong to repair?"

"No. Why would you think that?"

She looked around the room, at the gutted odd-colored candles and the empty wine bottle—at the dishes that wouldn't be cleaned because there was no water with which to wash them. So many little things wrong—just like all the little things wrong with their marriage. "I've spent all week trying to make things perfect between us," she said. "And I keep failing."

"Things don't have to be perfect." He leaned closer and clasped both her hands now. "People aren't perfect, so how could a marriage ever be?"

She nodded, remembering Albert's words that marriage wasn't about perfection, but about hard work. "What are we going to do?" she whispered.

"Whatever it takes." He bent and kissed her hand, then stayed that way, his forehead pressed against her knee. She was struck by the humbleness of the posture, of all the feeling in that one gesture. Tentatively, she freed one hand and stroked his hair. There was more gray there than she'd realized before and it was thinner than she remembered, but still precious to her.

She wasn't sure if she should give in to his plea that they try again. Hadn't she already tried so much? Would things really get better, or would this only prolong the inevitable? Charles was a certain kind of man—strong and silent and reserved. He'd been perfect for her once, but now she needed more—maybe more than he could give.

She felt a dampness on her knee and her hand stilled. He was shaking now, a barely perceptible tremor in his shoulders, and she realized he was crying. Her silent, stoic husband was weeping at the thought of losing her.

Something in her broke and she bent her body over his, embracing him and adding her tears to his own. "We'll try again," she whispered, stroking his back. "We'll try and try until we figure out how to get it right."

TASIA WAS NOT ONE for preparing elaborate meals. That is what restaurants were for. But she made an exception for this lunch with her son. She wanted to talk with Theo in private and she had persuaded him to visit her in her home in Athens before he returned to the United States. She had deigned to prepare salad niçoise to serve with the rolls she'd purchased from the bakery and a bottle of red wine. For dessert there was amygdalopita, the almond brandy cake that was Theo's particular favorite.

"Very nice, Mother," he said, surveying the table as he held out her chair for her. "What's the occasion?"

"I wanted to have luncheon with my son." She unfurled her napkin and spread it in her lap while Theo took the seat across from her. "How have you been?"

"I've been well," he said, still eyeing her cautiously. Really, where did he get this tendency to suspicion? Certainly not from *her*.

"And how have you been?" Theo asked, playing the role of dutiful son.

"My business interests keep me occupied," she said. Her work as a collection consultant for an Athens museum was pleasant, but not particularly challenging, or financially rewarding. All the more reason to cultivate outside interests. Some of those interests had required too much of her attention of late, but that would soon change. In a few short weeks—days, really—she would not worry about that anymore. She'd be able to retire to the life of luxury she'd been denied too long.

She helped herself to the salad and passed the platter to Theo. "How was your lunch with your father yesterday?" she asked, her tone casual.

Theo's eyes narrowed. "It was a good lunch."

She waited for him to elaborate, but he did not. He was deliberately teasing her. Didn't he know how much this particular lunch interested her? "Tell me about it," she prompted.

"We ate at my friend Stephen's new place. I had the lamb."

She stabbed at a piece of tuna, no longer bothering to hide her irritation. "And how was Elias? Was he looking well?"

"Very well. He seems happier than I've seen him before."

"No doubt he's thrilled at the success of his new cruise line." The thought pleased her. The more content Elias was with his success now, the more satisfying it would be when he was brought down later.

"I'm sure he is. *Alexandra's Dream* is doing very

well. But I don't believe that's the reason for this particular happiness." Theo broke off a bit of bread and chewed slowly, then washed it down with a long drink of wine. "The luncheon is very good, Mother," he said. "Where did you find the tuna? It's very fresh. Did you go to Marco's or the new place near the square?"

She wasn't going to be sidetracked by a discussion of the merits of one fish market over another. "I don't remember where I got it. It's not important." She doubted Theo had any real interest in buying fresh tuna. He only wanted to keep her in suspense. "To what do you attribute Elias's newfound happiness?" she asked.

"I believe it might have to do with the woman who accompanied him to our lunch," Theo said, not suppressing a smile.

"A woman?" Tasia sat up straighter. This *was* news. "What woman was that?" No doubt he'd found some twentysomething model or starlet to adorn his arm. Such attachments were practically a cliché with men his age, weren't they? True, since Alexandra's death, Elias had been amazingly discrete, but she supposed his true nature was bound to come out eventually.

"I told you he was seeing Sadie Bennett," Theo said.

Tasia almost choked on her wine. She coughed, but quickly recovered. "The librarian's mother?" *Derek Bennett's widow?*

When Theo had mentioned Ariana's mother before, Tasia had been sure Elias only wanted to get rid of the troublemaking woman, not become involved in a relationship with her.

"Yes. I see you do remember." He smiled. "They seem quite taken with each other."

"What's she like?" Tasia asked, throwing aside all pretext of being uninterested. She had long wondered about Sadie. Of course, for years she had only known her as Derek's wife, seldom alluded to and never seen.

When Derek and Tasia had first met, he had been honest with her about his marriage, telling her he had a child and, therefore, no intention of leaving his wife. Since she had no desire to marry, this had suited Tasia fine. With little effort on the part of either of them, their working relationship had evolved to a more personal level. They had had many good years together, unmarred by any thought of his wife.

Then Derek had died. In addition to jeopardizing Tasia's very profitable business, his death had left a hole in her life she had not anticipated. She missed her lover and had many tender thoughts of him. For the first time, she resented the fact that some other woman might also mourn him.

Then his daughter, Ariana, had showed up to interfere for who-knows-what reason. Sadie had followed—and why? Were these women determined to plague her? To interfere with her plans? Or even to demand a share of the money her association with Derek had brought to her?

"I can't imagine what she's doing here," she said out loud. "You'd think a woman whose husband had recently died would be home, in mourning, instead of taking a cruise."

"Sadie Bennett's husband has been dead ten

months," Theo said. "And her daughter is missing. I believe she's on the cruise in hopes of learning something about Ariana's whereabouts."

Tasia dismissed the idea. "The girl has run off with some man she met in Naples," she said. "Isn't that what everyone is saying?"

"It's what some people are saying. Others don't believe it's true."

"I certainly don't care anything about her." Tasia poked her fork among the lettuce and tuna remaining on her plate. "Her mother should go home."

"Why are you so interested in Sadie Bennett?" Theo asked. "Or in Elias, for that matter?"

She pushed her plate away. "I only want to know what kind of woman could hold Elias's interest after his sainted Alexandra's death."

"I think Elias truly cares for Mrs. Bennett," Theo said.

Tasia doubted this. Elias didn't have a caring bone in his body. If anything or anyone interfered with his plans for his life they were discarded, as she and Theo had once been cast aside without so much as a second thought.

"Where is the ship going next?" she asked, ostensibly changing the subject. "Will you be conducting more tours for Elias's passengers soon?"

"The next port is Sorrento, then they'll go back to Piraeus for a final short cruise around the Greek Isles," he said. "From there, they move to the Caribbean. I won't have any more business from them this season."

She nodded. "You do well enough on your own. You

needn't depend on him to support you. Good thing, since he never has."

Theo frowned at her, but said nothing more. The rest of the meal was finished in strained silence. Theo declined the amygdalopita and stood. "I have to go now, Mother," he said. "I'll see you in a few months."

After a dutiful kiss on her cheek, he departed. She left the dishes on the table and took a glass of wine into her bedroom, where she paced the floor, her emotions in a turmoil.

What was Elias up to? How much did Sadie know and how much had she told Elias? Would she ruin everything Tasia had been so carefully setting up for months now?

The thought was too bitter to bear. She had worked too hard—risked too much—to allow one interfering woman—one who had, after all, taken so much from her already—to destroy everything.

She emptied the wineglass and set it aside, then strode to the phone. If she was going to pull this off, she was obviously going to have to take a more personal interest. Even better, she could be on board *Alexandra's Dream* when her plan to bring Elias down came to fruition.

She could picture it now—Elias's indignation when authorities came to search the ship. His protestations of innocence when they found the stolen artifacts. All deference and respect vanishing from the officers' manner when they found the papers linking the artifacts to Elias. Elias being led away in handcuffs, past the horrified stares of passengers and his family.

Would his new love weep at the idea? Or curse him for lying to her?

Remembering Sadie made Tasia think of Ariana. Although the men she had hired had done an excellent job of getting the girl out of the way, Tasia could admit to a certain curiosity about Derek's daughter. Was she anything like her father? And how much did she know about his activities?

She picked up the phone and punched in a number. "This is Megaera," she said when a man answered. "I want to go to Vathi."

She paused, listening intently.

"Yes. At once. Then I'll need you to take me to Piraeus." She smiled to herself, anticipation warming her like fine brandy. "I'm going on a cruise."

CHAPTER SIXTEEN

SADIE WONDERED WHY she had waited so long to travel. As she sat at a small table outside the coffee shop and watched the play of golden sunlight on azure sea and felt the warm sea breeze caress her, she regretted all the years she'd wasted not venturing out to see this kind of glory.

While Derek had traveled the world in search of antiquities to add to his museum's collection, she had waited at home, suppressing her envy of his freedom, telling herself it was her duty to stay behind to care for their home and their child. She had listened to his tales of historic cities and amazing sights and told herself she was content without such things in her life.

Such a lie. She should have taken Ariana with her to see the world. If Derek had not allowed them to accompany him, they could have gone on their own. How much it would have meant to her now to know she had shared beauty like this with her daughter. As the days passed, it was getting more and more difficult to cling to the hope that she would ever see Ariana again.

She fought not to let such thoughts take root, but her mind insisted on returning to these worries, even in the midst of paradise.

"I hate to see such a beautiful woman looking so sad." Elias stopped beside her table.

She glanced up, unable even in her sadness to keep back a smile for him. "Good morning," she said. "It's hard to believe a real place could be as gorgeous as this." She looked out once more at the sea. "I've never seen such an amazing shade of blue."

He nodded. "May I join you?"

"Please do." Having Elias with her would only make the morning more perfect.

"You're thinking about Ariana," he said.

She nodded. Not a difficult thing to guess, but she appreciated his acknowledgment of her concern. "I know worrying doesn't help," she said. "But I can't stop."

"I know." He leaned back in his chair. "It's part of being a parent. Women may show it more, but fathers have just as many fears. The moment the doctor put my daughters in my arms, I started worrying about how to protect them, how to ensure their happiness."

"You've been a good father, I'm sure." She gave him another smile. "Katherine certainly turned out well. But come to think of it, I haven't seen her since the memorial service for June. Is she all right?"

"Yes. She and Charles slipped away for a couple of days in the French countryside. A second honeymoon."

She laughed. "I'm thinking only a cruise ship owner's daughter would need a vacation from a vacation like this."

He smiled. "Katherine and Charles both have a hard time leaving their work behind. On board ship, Katherine still feels responsible for things like June's service. And, with roughly a thousand passengers and half again as many crew members, it's difficult to ever be truly alone here."

And, yet, before she had met Elias, she had felt terribly alone, even in a crowd of people. "I hope they have a wonderful time."

"I do, too. They need this time away. Every couple does. Otherwise, life gets too much in the way of love. At least that's what I tried to tell her when I urged her to take this cruise in the first place." He shook his head. "Katherine thinks I meddle too much."

"Do you?" she teased.

"Maybe. I'm used to being in charge." His gaze met hers, his eyes dark and solemn. "Does that bother you?"

"If it does, I'll tell you."

"Promise?"

The one word hinted at so much—at a future that held the possibility of him wanting to know the truth about her feelings. "Of course," she murmured, and looked out at the ocean once more.

He joined her in contemplating the view and neither of them spoke for some minutes. It was a comfortable silence, though Sadie was acutely aware of his presence beside her. Just being with him filled her with such contentment.

"Whenever I am in this part of the world, I wonder why I ever leave," he said after a while.

She tore her eyes from the sea and turned to look at him—an equally pleasant view. Younger women might laugh at the idea, but she had grown to treasure the fine lines fanning out from the corners of his eyes and mouth and the silver at his temples. These were the badges of life well lived, the marks of time spent in the sun and wind out of doors and of much time smiling.

He met her gaze and his appreciative look warmed her through. "I'm going to especially hate for this cruise to be over," he said.

"Yesterday I made reservations for the next sailing," she told him.

"Because you're enjoying yourself so much?"

"Partly that, and partly because I can't bear to leave without Ariana." She stared out at the sea again. "I may be deluding myself, but I feel she's close. Have you heard anything more from your detective?"

"No. No one had heard of this Dante person before he came to work on the diggings and no one has seen him since."

"Or Ariana."

"Or Ariana." He squeezed her hand. "I won't rest until we find something, I promise."

Amazing how much comfort could be conveyed in a simple touch. Of course, Elias's touches had ceased being simple to her days ago. After being alone for so long, even through the years of her marriage, she found it wonderful to have someone else share her worries.

"I wish I could come on the next sailing with you," he said. "Unfortunately, I must return to Athens. I've already stayed away from work too long."

Pain squeezed her heart. She'd known this moment was coming, but had hoped to put it off as long as possible. "I'll miss you," she said, withdrawing her hand from his.

He turned toward her, leaning forward, only the small table between them. "I know this isn't the best time to discuss this," he said. "I know your mind is on Ariana and her whereabouts, but I want to continue seeing you. A great deal of you."

Her heart fluttered and she had trouble catching her breath. "I…I want to see you, too," she stammered.

"After Alexandra died, I told myself I had loved one good woman and that was enough," he said. "I had a family and a business to look after. Romance was for the young and I didn't need it. You showed me how wrong I was."

"I sometimes wonder if Derek and I were ever really in love," she said. "I believe we truly cared for one another, but there was a distance between us we could never bridge." She glanced at him. "I told myself it was just that way with men and women, but I've never felt that distance with you."

He held out his hand again and she took it. "I don't know what I would have done these past few days if you hadn't been here," she continued. "You have been such a great comfort to me."

"I like to think your feelings go beyond gratitude," he said.

"They do. But gratitude is certainly part of them."

"I want Ariana to be found safely," he said. "She's a lovely young woman and I feel partly responsible for her, since she was working for me when she disappeared. But I'll confess, I have an ulterior motive for wanting her safe return. I want you happy and to have you all to myself."

He leaned forward and kissed her, a gentle brush of his lips that nevertheless sent heat curling to her toes. She wondered if it was possible to have another person "all to yourself," but she would like to try with Elias.

"When do you have to leave?" she asked.

"Tomorrow, when we return to Piraeus. But I'll stay in touch. Do you have e-mail?"

She nodded. A computer would be a poor substitute for a flesh-and-blood man, but a little time apart might give her the opportunity to think through her feelings for him. Even at her age, she wasn't sure she knew what it was to be in love. But she was certain her feelings for Elias were as close to the real thing as she'd come yet.

KATHERINE AND CHARLES sat side by side in the dining room of the villa, holding hands and not speaking, as the sun crept toward noon. "What do we do now?" she asked, her voice seeming loud in the room that had been silent so long.

"We could open another bottle of wine," Charles said.

She shook her head. "No. I've had too much already." A dull pain throbbed behind her eyes. "What I'd really like is a bath," she said. Knowing she couldn't have one made her long for it all the more.

"I might be able to help you with that," he said. A half smile formed on his lips.

"Don't tease me, Charles," she scolded. "Not when I feel so wretched."

"I'm not teasing. Come on." He stood and pulled her to her feet, also. "While I was walking this morning, I noticed there's a pond behind us."

"A pond? You mean, like a goldfish pond?" She shuddered. The idea of bathing with fish and who knew what other creatures definitely did not appeal.

"Not a fish pond. There's a stream and part of it is dammed off." He tugged her toward the door.

He led her through the kitchen and onto the back stoop. She looked in the direction he indicated and caught the glimmer of silvery water in the sunlight. A willow tree leaned over the water, its dark branches reflected in the still surface. A stone bench sat beside it, a silent invitation to linger.

"Come on, let's take a look," he said.

Hand in hand, they crossed the expanse of rough ground to the pond. The dark water was placid, undisturbed by fish or sea monsters or other undesirables. "It looks wonderful," she said. She kicked off her sandals and dabbled one foot in the water. It was just cool enough without being cold. "Too bad I left our swimsuits on board the ship," she said wistfully. She'd actually packed very few clothes at all for their two nights away. She'd hoped they'd be too busy in bed to have time to swim.

"Who needs swimsuits?" He grinned and began unbuttoning his shirt. "It's surrounded by trees and there's no one else around. And, if anyone does see us, they'll dismiss us as a pair of crazy tourists."

She burst out laughing. "Skinny-dipping?" Her quiet, reserved husband baring it all like a teenager? Not to mention expecting her to join him?

"Why not?" He pulled off the shirt and unbuckled his belt. "Last one in is a rotten egg."

She watched in amazement as his pants followed his shirt, tossed aside on the ground, and felt an insistent tickle of desire. The sun burnished his skin and high-lighted the definition of muscle in his chest and shoulders. Her husband was still a very handsome man.

"What's the matter?" he asked, one hand on the waistband of his boxers.

"Charles, I've never seen you like this," she said.

"Then, it's about time you did." He took her hand. "You said you wanted this trip to be a chance for us to get close again. To get to know each other again. We can start with this."

His words inspired her. If Charles was willing to let go of his reserve for this, then how could she hold back from joining him? She unbuttoned her blouse and quickly shed it and the linen capris she'd worn and reached around to unfasten the clasp of her bra.

When they were both naked, Charles turned and dived into the water. A sudden breeze chilled her and she stood on the bank, arms hugged around her breasts, feeling awkward and vulnerable.

Charles surfaced and slicked back his hair. "What's the matter?" he asked.

She shrugged. "I guess I'm nervous."

"Don't be." He offered his hand. "Hold on to me so you don't slip."

Feeling foolish, she bent and grasped his hand. The next thing she knew, she was pulled into the water. She squealed and landed with a splash, his arms around her.

"That was a dirty trick!" she said, slapping at him and slipping from his grasp.

He reached for her, but she skipped away. Laughing and splashing, they moved around the small pond, Katherine always keeping a few inches ahead of him. The sensation of cool water and cooler air against her naked skin awakened every nerve and heightened all her senses. She felt young and alive and freer than she had in years.

With a mighty lunge, Charles surged forward and captured her. "I've got you now," he shouted in triumph. He laughed and pulled her tighter against him, his erection hot against her stomach.

She was out of breath from both exertion and arousal. Feeling bold, she wrapped her legs around him, her thighs tight against his, her hands wrapped around his upper arms. "Now who has whom?" she teased.

He walked backward with her into deeper water, beneath the arching tree. The water was cooler here, sliding like silk against their fevered skin, an erotic caress. Charles leaned closer and kissed her, the kiss of a lover, claiming her with lips and tongue, stealing breath and voice and awareness of anything but the feel of his body clinging to hers.

When, at last he broke the kiss, he looked into her eyes, his hands smoothing up and down her back. "You're amazing," he said. "I don't think I stop and appreciate that nearly enough."

"That's what this moment is all about," she said. "Doing things we haven't done nearly enough of."

"Skinny-dipping?" There was laughter in his voice, though his eyes remained serious.

"That, and making love whenever and wherever we

feel like it. Being wild and carefree and maybe even a little irresponsible." Heaven knew they'd both been so, *so* responsible all their lives. "Maybe you have to be a little more mature to know how important those things are," she said.

He nodded. "Breaking the rules when you're young isn't as much fun because you don't fully realize how much you're getting away with."

"You could look at it that way." She smoothed her hand along his shoulder. "But, really, I didn't care so much about this kind of freedom when I was younger," she said. "I loved being a wife and a mother and the responsibility of it all. But now I'm older and other people's opinions and prescribed roles don't mean as much to me. I want to try new things—to be daring. But I want you to be daring with me."

"Are you saying I'm not daring?"

She couldn't keep back a startled laugh. "Charles! You always do the proper thing at the proper time."

He made a face. "You're saying I'm boring."

"Staid. Conventional. Very respectable."

"Boring." He grasped her thighs and adjusted her against him.

She giggled. "Well, you're certainly not being boring now."

"You've jarred me out of my rut. And why not? Now that Gemma is grown and our businesses are well established, why not take a few more breaks? A few more risks?"

"And be more daring?" She traced a drop of water down his neck across his chest.

"Yes, more daring." He slid his hand up to cup her breast and dragged his thumb across her nipple. Desire lanced through her and she tightened her thighs around him.

They began to move together in a weightless dance. Her hands slid over his slick skin, exploring, rediscovering all the places she loved—the hollow of his shoulder, the ridges of his spine, the jut of his hip bone. His mouth and tongue traced kisses along her throat, along her collarbone and around her breasts. All the while, he supported her against him, his hands kneading her bottom and thighs.

When she was panting and needy, unable to bear waiting a moment more, he slid into her, fitting her firmly against him, then beginning to move in a dance that was as familiar to her as breathing and, yet, in this moment, brand-new. It was a magical moment, a kind of baptism for their newfound commitment to each other.

"I love you, Charles!" she shouted as she climaxed. The words held more meaning now than they ever had before, when she'd come so close to throwing them away. Together, they would rediscover all the things they had treasured about one another over the years, and make their bond stronger than ever. The love they shared was perfect, even if she and Charles were not.

EPILOGUE

As Katherine and Charles stepped onto the deck of *Alexandra's Dream* in Sorrento, she felt almost like a newlywed. Certainly there was that same sense of anticipation, of a life filled with a hundred possibilities and of depths of love waiting to be discovered.

Hand in hand, they were greeted by her father. "You two look well rested from your little getaway," Elias said after he'd kissed Katherine's cheek and shook Charles's hand. "I take it the villa was nice."

"The villa was horrible," Charles said. He smiled at Katherine, and she bit back a laugh, remembering just how horrible—and how wonderful—the villa had been. "But, when you're with the right person, the surroundings don't matter so much."

Elias beamed. "Glad to hear it. Very glad to hear it." He turned to Charles. "Why don't you take your things to your quarters while I have a word with my daughter."

Charles's eyes met hers once more, communicating that he knew exactly what Elias was up to, but that he didn't mind. He kissed her lightly on the lips. "Join me as soon as you can," he whispered, the urgency in his voice sending a warm thrill up her spine.

When they were alone, Elias led Katherine along the rail. "Well?" he asked.

"Well, what?" She assumed a mysterious smile.

"Have the two of you patched things up? No more talk of divorce?"

"We talked a lot." *In between making love round the clock.* "When we return home, we're going to see a counselor, and Charles has agreed to rearrange his work schedule so he isn't away from home as much. I'm hopeful things are going to work out for us." These past two days, she had remembered all the reasons she married Charles and why, despite his flaws and her own faults, he really was the perfect man for her.

"I'm glad." He put his arm around her. "I know you think I was sticking my nose where it didn't belong, but all I ever wanted was to see you happy."

"I know. And I'm glad you suggested this getaway. You were right. The thing we needed most was time alone together, to get to know each other again."

"That's the best news you could have had for me."

"Now it's my turn to be nosy," she said. "What's going on with you and Sadie Bennett?"

He patted her hand. "What makes you think something is going on between me and Mrs. Bennett?"

"I've seen you together. You can't take your eyes off each other. I haven't known you to pay so much attention to any woman since Mother died."

He nodded. "Nothing is settled until she finds her daughter, but I'm hopeful, too, that she and I will be seeing a great deal more of each other in the future." He glanced at her, his expression serious. "I hope you can accept Sadie. No woman will ever replace your mother, but I'm tired of being alone, and I appreciate another opportunity for love."

Her breath caught at the word *love*. Things were even more serious than she had suspected. But she couldn't remember when he'd looked happier. She had always thought of him as such a strong, independent person, and the knowledge that he had been lonely made her regret her assumptions. "I'm happy for you," she said. "Truly. I worried at first, but everything I've been through with Charles has made me realize there are a lot of paths to love and not all of them are smooth."

"I'm glad. Your disapproval wouldn't stop me from seeing her, but I'm much happier with your blessing."

"I like Sadie. I've liked her from the moment I met her." She hesitated. "You're sure she had nothing to do with her husband's smuggling activities?"

"The police aren't even certain her husband was involved, since he died before they could complete their investigation. But I'm convinced Sadie knew nothing about anything Derek was up to. From what she tells me, it was a rather distant relationship." He stopped and his eyes met hers again. "You have your mother's habit of worrying about everything, but remember that I'm not a naive young man. One of the reasons I've remained unattached so long is that I don't trust easily."

She nodded. "Good. She didn't seem like the type to be involved in something like that, but for your sake, I wanted to be sure."

They resumed their stroll along the railing. A stiff breeze blew off the starboard side this afternoon and Katherine wondered if they were in for a storm.

"Sadie is going to stay on for the final cruise before *Alexandra's Dream* sails for the Caribbean," Elias said after a moment. "I have to return to Athens, but she and I have agreed to remain in touch. I'm hoping I can convince her to visit me at my home soon."

"Has there been any more news of Ariana's whereabouts?"

"None." He dropped his head. "I have a bad feeling about the girl. Sadie says she's had dreams that Ariana is in trouble."

"What could have happened to her?"

"The Camorra are known to be involved in several of the digs in Paestum, where she was last seen. If she stumbled onto something she wasn't supposed to have seen, they wouldn't have hesitated to kill her."

Katherine shuddered. "I pray that hasn't happened."

"I do, too, for her sake as well as for her mother's. Sadie and Ariana were very close. Like you and Gemma."

Katherine nodded. "I don't know what I'd do if anything ever happened to Gemma."

He squeezed her shoulder. "You'd go on. It's what we all do. And what Sadie will do, with my help." He took his arm away and inhaled deeply of the sea air. "Why are we talking of such dreary subjects? We're doing everything we can to find Ariana and Gemma is doing well at school, isn't she?"

"Yes. From the sound of her e-mails, she's enjoying it very much." Before leaving for the villa, Katherine had had another, longer e-mail from Gemma. The "hot guy" was named Todd, and Gemma had met him at a soccer game. He was a premed student. They'd gone to the movies once and "hung out" with friends. Not a great many details, but enough to reassure Katherine that her daughter still wanted to confide in her.

"Then, you don't have anything to worry about," Elias said. "You can put all your energy into enjoying this next phase of your marriage. I can tell you, after you and your sister left home, your mother and I were closer than ever. It was like being newlyweds all over again, with more money and more sense."

Katherine laughed. "I don't know about that, but there's something to be said for falling in love again with someone you've known half your life."

"That's because the two of you are perfect for each other," he said. "I've always known it, even if you couldn't see it."

"No one is perfect," she said. "And neither is any marriage. I made a mistake thinking something was wrong with mine because it didn't live up to the impossible fantasies in my head."

"Part of love is accepting each other's flaws," Elias said. "Knowing someone loves you in spite of everything that's wrong with you is a great gift."

"Yes, it is." She leaned over and kissed his cheek. "I'd better go now. Charles is waiting. And I don't want to waste another minute of this vacation apart from him." She and Charles still had healing to do, but she had no doubt they'd be stronger now than they'd ever been before. And perfectly in love in spite of—and because of—their imperfections.

* * * * *

MEDITERRANEAN NIGHTS
Join the glamorous world of cruising with
the guests and crew of Alexandra's Dream—*the*
newest luxury ship to set sail on the romantic
Mediterranean.
The voyage continues in January 2008 with
FULL EXPOSURE
by Diana Duncan

Ariana Bennett, the unassuming librarian
of *Alexandra's Dream,* is more than she seems.
She's on a mission to clear her late father's name
from charges of antiquities theft. But, while trying
to infiltrate the underworld of antiquities smuggling,
she finds herself held captive with a mysterious
stranger—Dante. In order to survive, they must
join forces. But Ariana wonders if she can really
trust him and, as her attraction for Dante grows,
she wonders if she can trust herself.

Here's a preview!

SHE TRIED TO MOVE. Her wrists, bound behind her back, throbbed in tandem with the pulsating heartbeat of twin engines. Her head pounded. Every breath dragged in her parched throat and her body felt as battered as a discarded piñata.

Like many foolish souls before her, she had challenged the fates—and lost. She moaned. She would rather have remained in the grip of somnolence. Oblivion was safer.

"Signorina Bennett?" The resonant baritone flavored with a rich Italian accent echoed from the abyss. "You are awake?"

She jerked. She wasn't dead.

But she hadn't escaped the devil.

"Where are you?" His deep voice in the black void seduced her with the promise of warmth. Compelled her to reply.

She compressed her lips. If he didn't know, she wasn't drawing him a map.

"Are you alright?"

That depended on the definition of *alright*. Surviving a mob kidnapping, yacht explosion, failed escape attempt and near drowning probably qualified. If she were a cat, she'd be eight lives short and counting.

"*Ariana?* It's Dante."

A shiver glided up her spine. As if she wouldn't recognize the alluring voice of a man who had her held hostage for almost six weeks.

At the end of August, an antiques dealer in the Naples market had directed her to a nearby archaeological dig. She'd found Dante excavating the site. A fierce, dark, *napoletano* with a big, hard-muscled body and spine-tingling voice. She'd asked a few questions, and the mob had kidnapped her. She'd been interrogated and almost killed by Dante's partner. Then she'd been drugged and had awoken in a strange house. Alone with Dante.

"Answer me, *bella.* I am also a prisoner."

She peered into the oily gloom. That was a new tactic. Fragmented memories of the previous night tumbled into place. Was this an elaborate plan to gain her cooperation? Signor Dante had held her captive for a month before bringing her aboard a yacht. They'd drifted around the Mediterranean nearly two more weeks. Yesterday, a fiery explosion had destroyed the yacht and, in the melee, she had been forced to rely on Dante to get her to shore. She'd tried to escape from him, but a few bullets from a guy in a Zodiac and they'd both ended up prisoners.

"We must act. We may not have much time before they return."

They? He actually sounded concerned. If this was a ruse, he'd done a superlative job. If their predicament *was* real, who would cross the mob by attacking him? Unless he wasn't working with the Camorra, Naples's Mafia. Perhaps the Camorra had hunted Dante down and incinerated the yacht. She closed her eyes. Impossible to think with a hammering headache.

Maybe Dante had gone rogue and kidnapped her solo. That would explain why he hadn't hurt her. She was his investment. It also explained why she hadn't been ransomed. Dante labored under the misimpression her family owned valuable antiques, although she'd explained many times that they were less solvent than dot com investors.

"Trust me," his low tone coaxed.

Right. And he had a cactus farm in Venice for sale. She cautiously shifted on the ice-cold floor, and her abused muscles shrieked. *Were* they both prisoners of the mob?

"Trust me, Ariana," he repeated fervently.

Even before Dante had kidnapped her, she'd felt so alone. So isolated. Her mother disapproved of her job on the ship, and Ariana hadn't been able to disclose the truth about her mission. Her father's former contacts were leery of her motives. Ariana had made friends among the cruise staff, but she couldn't confide in them about her plans to clear her father's name. And she was suspicious of two employees who had expressed a little too much interest in her. The priest was savvy about antiquities and gave lectures to the passengers in the library, but Father Connelly's disposition wasn't exactly saintly. And First Officer Giorgio Tzekas was a player.

She wanted desperately to trust in something—trust *someone*. Dante had not threatened or hurt her. He'd calmly refuted her fear that he meant her harm, and remained cool and aloof…while implacably refusing to release her.

"I know you are listening, *signorina*. Why won't you answer?"

How did he know? She gnawed at her lower lip. Logic had failed during her five-month journey to restore her father's reputation. She'd gotten nowhere. A woman of order and reason, she had been thrust into an alien universe.

"San Gennaro, mio bello, aiutami!" Distress tinged his muttered exclamation. "If you wish to live, speak!"

REQUEST YOUR
FREE BOOKS!

2 FREE NOVELS
PLUS 2
FREE GIFTS!

YES! Please send me 2 FREE Harlequin Presents® novels and my 2 FREE gifts. After receiving them, if I don't wish to receive any more books, I can return the shipping statement marked "cancel." If I don't cancel, I will receive 6 brand-new novels every month and be billed just $3.80 per book in the U.S., or $4.47 per book in Canada, plus 25¢ shipping and handling per book and applicable taxes, if any*. That's a savings of close to 15% off the cover price! I understand that accepting the 2 free books and gifts places me under no obligation to buy anything. I can always return a shipment and cancel at any time. Even if I never buy another book from Harlequin, the two free books and gifts are mine to keep forever.

106 HDN EEXK   306 HDN EEXV

Name	(PLEASE PRINT)	
Address		Apt. #
City	State/Prov.	Zip/Postal Code

Signature (if under 18, a parent or guardian must sign)

Mail to the **Harlequin Reader Service®:**
IN U.S.A.: P.O. Box 1867, Buffalo, NY 14240-1867
IN CANADA: P.O. Box 609, Fort Erie, Ontario L2A 5X3

Not valid to current Harlequin Presents subscribers.

Want to try two free books from another line?
Call 1-800-873-8635 or visit www.morefreebooks.com.

* Terms and prices subject to change without notice. NY residents add applicable sales tax. Canadian residents will be charged applicable provincial taxes and GST. This offer is limited to one order per household. All orders subject to approval. Credit or debit balances in a customer's account(s) may be offset by any other outstanding balance owed by or to the customer. Please allow 4 to 6 weeks for delivery.

Your Privacy: Harlequin is committed to protecting your privacy. Our Privacy Policy is available online at www.eHarlequin.com or upon request from the Reader Service. From time to time we make our lists of customers available to reputable firms who may have a product or service of interest to you. If you would prefer we not share your name and address, please check here. ☐

HP0

nocturne™

Jachin Black always knew he was an outcast.
Not only was he a vampire, he was a vampire
banished from the Sanguinas society. Jachin, forced
to survive among mortals, is determined to buy
his way back into the clan one day.

Ariel Swanson, debut author of a vampire novel, could
be the ticket he needs to get revenge and take his
rightful place among the Sanguinas again. However,
the unsuspecting mortal woman has no idea of the
dark and sensual path she will be forced to travel.

Look for

RESURRECTION: THE BEGINNING

by

PATRICE MICHELLE

Available January 2008 wherever you buy books.

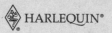

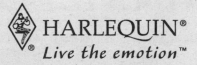